I0684423

The Disperser
a werewolf novel

by Matthew Alan Hughes

Disperser – "A wolf that leaves the pack and strikes out on its own." from the International Wolf Center

The Disperser

MATTHEW ALAN HUGHES

ABOUT THE AUTHOR

"With a jeweler's eye for detail, a twisted sense of the macabre, and the nose of a newspaperman, Matthew Alan Hughes is a fantasist to watch. He knows how to keep a heart palpitating, and a reader up well past their bedtime. Check this guy out – highly recommended!" - Jay Bonansinga, the New York Times bestselling author of THE WALKING DEAD: DESCENT and BLOOD SAMPLES

This is for everyone who has believed in me and supported me through the years!

Prologue

In the bathroom of a small dive hotel, Steve Slate knelt beside the bathtub and gently rubbed soap into his little girl's hair. Miranda was playing with a toy fish and trying to ignore the assault on her head. The three year old loved bath time, she just hated getting a bath. Especially getting her hair washed. To her bath time, like any other time, was just another excuse to play. To her the bathtub was just a private, indoor swimming pool.

"Hold still," he said as he used the complimentary Styrofoam coffee cup to rinse soap from her hair. Then he ran a comb through it, trying to get all of the knots and tangles out. Steve knew very little about caring for a little girl or her hair, but he could remember a few of the things that Chloe had told him. She had said you always needed to comb the tangles out while her hair was still wet.

"Ouch, quit it," Miranda protested. She swiped at the comb with the little hand that clutched the fish.

"Hold on a second Mir," he said, using his free hand to hold her hair in an attempt not to pull it. "And don't swing at me."

"Sorry daddy," she said, sticking out her bottom lip. It was her patented move, but no matter how many times he saw it, it always got him.

"It's okay, honey, just don't do it again," Steve warned,

"Daddy, will you be a monster?" Miranda asked.

"A monster?"

"Yes, will you be a monster?"

He laughed, but felt the sound catch in his throat. It brought reality back to him quicker than he had hoped. They needed to get moving. He still had eleven hours to drive before he would be at his brother's house in Missouri, and he absolutely had to be there before dark. He

1

had no choice, not since he had Miranda with him. He had messed up a lot of things during his life, but that was one mistake he could not make.

"Please, daddy!"

"Honey, we really have to go," Steve told her. "Uncle Rick is waiting for us to get to his house."

"Just one time," she pleaded and the lip came out again.

Steve sighed. He knew he couldn't win. Miranda was a good kid, not like a lot of the other spoilt brats he'd seen at Walmart and other places. But sometime she got something into her little head and wasn't going to be satisfied until she got it. This was one of those times, but it was partially his fault. He had started the game over a year ago when they were still a normal family, with a father, mother and daughter. Chloe had just rolled her eyes, thinking he was being stupid, but it was all part of the father-daughter bonding thing. It was something the two of them shared.

"Okay, one time and then you're getting your little bottom out of the tub."

"Thanks daddy," she said with a smile, and for just a moment all of his doubts and fears faded away.

He held his right hand up in the air like a mouth and made a roaring sound. Miranda pretended to be scared and squealed in a mixture of fear and delight. He opened and closed the monster's "mouth" and moved it towards her head. She giggled and ducked as far away from him as she could get. He held back his own laughter and roared again, which brought about another round of squealing. Then the monster bit at her hair and Miranda pointed at his hand with one little finger.

"No, bad monster," she said. "Drink water, don't eat people."

"But I'm hungry," he said in a bad cartoon mon-

2

ster voice.

"I sorry monster," she said, faking a sad face. "Eating people is...not...nice."

"Just one bite?"

"No, no, no, no."

"Just a little, please."

Miranda took the cup he had been using to wash her hair and scooped up some soapy water. She put it in front of "the monster" and smiled. His hand pretended to look from her to the cup, and then dove into it, splashing water all over and making his daughter giggle. After a minute he couldn't help it, he started laughing too.

An hour after checking out of their hotel, they were crossing the Mississippi River into Missouri. He had wanted to show Miranda the big river, but she had drifted off to sleep in her car seat on the passenger side of his truck. She looked so sweet and innocent that he couldn't bring himself to wake her. So he turned his attention back to the road and drove.

The flat countryside of eastern Missouri flew by almost as fast as the minutes. They were still two hours away from his brother's house with just over two hours until dark. He still wasn't sure how all of this worked. He didn't know if the change would take him as soon as it got dark, or if he would have a little time to drop her off and get away.

Only two days ago he had thought he had everything figured out. Life made sense. But the last two days had been a blur. From the moment he stepped out of Owen's truck in that field, everything he knew about life had ceased to make sense.

He looked at Miranda sleeping quietly in her car seat and felt a cold chill. His heart told him that he could never do anything to hurt her. But two days ago he would have said the same about Chloe. The image of her with glowing eyes and sharp gnashing teeth would forever be burned into his mind. He saw it every time he closed his eyes.

If she couldn't withstand the alpha's orders, he didn't stand a chance against the full moon. He had to get Miranda to safety.

He had called Rick, his brother, and told him that they were on the way, but he had no way of explaining things to him. He couldn't really tell his brother, "Hey, Chloe and I are werewolves now, so you're going to have to take care of Miranda for a while."

None of this was fair. Not to he and Chloe, but especially not to Miranda. She deserved to grow up in a home with two loving parents, not getting dropped off on her uncle's doorstep without ever knowing what had become of her parents. And he was pretty sure that would be the case. Whether he survived the full moon or not, no one would ever hear from him again. He was as good as dead.

PART ONE
The Hunted

Chapter One

Three Days Earlier

The first five years of their marriage had been perfect. He and Chloe had been high school sweethearts, and had continued that love affair well into their marriage. Then Miranda had come along, taking their relationship to the next level. They were truly a family, and happy in every way possible. They had no worries about money or health. Everything had been perfect. Everything had been just the way they had always dreamed it would be. Then evil had crept into their lives and they had not known it until it was too late.

Even after it was all said and done, Steve still didn't know exactly how it had all played out. A new neighbor had moved into their quiet suburban neighborhood, a young, good looking guy with money. Owen was the type of guy everyone noticed. The women loved him because he was rich and attractive, the men liked him because he was a man's man. He loved to talk about hunting, and the walls of his living room were covered with the heads of animals that he had killed. He especially stressed how he ate everything he killed. He worked that into any conversation he had about hunting. He was the neighborhood's new handyman, and was always out in his yard working with his power tools.

When Owen had invited Steve to go hunting with him, he hadn't hesitated to accept the invitation. Steve had been a big hunter growing up but hadn't been in over a decade. He loved it, but life just seemed to get in the way. He usually pulled double shifts in the fall when his coworkers were all taking off to go deer hunting. He saved his vacation time to spend with his family and was more than happy with that arraigment.

That particular night Owen said they would be coon hunting. Steve had never been, but he'd known a

7

lot of guys who enjoyed the sport when he was in high school. It was one of the unofficial 'redneck sports'. They'd load the truck down with dogs, drive out to the middle of nowhere and spend the night splashing around in the mud. It had never appealed to him.

Steve was a little confused because Owen didn't have any dogs, but the young man assured him that a whole pack would meet them in the woods. So he dug some old boots and camo out of his closet, and met his neighbor in the drive.

"It's gonna be a great night," Owen had promised, but there was something different about him. A look in his eye. Steve tried to play it off, but his gut told him that something was wrong. The other man had a half crazed look about him, like he was either going out of his mind or had spent the day shooting up. "I just love a good hunt, don't you?"

"Sure," Steve had said.

They climbed into Owen's jacked-up four wheel drive and set off out of the neighborhood at twenty over the speed limit. Steve kept glancing over at the other man, who had a crooked smile playing across his lips. It triggered some ancient instinct in him that he didn't know he had. He played it cool but was on edge from the moment they pulled out of the driveway. He absently thumbed the silver cross he wore around his neck, which was a habit he had picked up not long after his mother had given it to him. His senses were as alert as they had ever been.

They finally arrived in a heavily wooded area, and Steve at once knew where they were. He lived in the city now, but he had grown up in a house not a mile away, straight through the trees and across a creek. He had spent his entire youth exploring these woods, and a

8

had once known every tree root and rock that lay from where they parked to his parents back door. At one time he could have walked that distance, almost with his eyes closed, but that had been more than a decade in the past.

"Where are the dogs?"

"Oh, they're here," Owen said, still smiling.

Steve climbed down from the truck, his hand frantically rubbing his cross. The night air was cool, and dew had settled on the tall grass. Overhead the sky was ablaze with what seemed like the largest face of the moon he had ever seen. If the field had been lit by street lights, it couldn't have been much brighter. He couldn't make out any sign of vehicles or dogs in any direction, just flowing grass that led all the way up to the edge of the forest.

"I don't see any dogs," Steve said.

The words were not even all the way out of his mouth when two figures rose from the grass not twenty yards away. It was eerie, the way that one minute they weren't there and the next they were. Both of them were large men, and they moved through the grass directly towards them. Even with the bright moonlight it was hard to make out their features, which were obscured by bushy black beards and long flowing hair.

"What is this?" he asked.

"It's my hunting party," Owen said, moving around the truck. "You see, I might have misled you a little, Steve. There is a pack here tonight, but they aren't dogs. At least not the type of dogs you were expecting."

As the moonlight hit the eyes of one of the approaching men, they shone red. Steve's breath caught in his throat. He had never been a superstitious man, and up until this point in his life he'd had little time for religion. But as he stood in the middle of the field that night, he said one of the first earnest prayers he had ever prayed. Even as he was praying, the modern, logical man inside

9

of him was trying to excuse what he saw, but his instincts were stronger. He knew what he was seeing wasn't a trick of the eye or a ruse meant to frighten him. These men were far worse than anything he had ever imagined existed.

"Let me explain the rules to you," Owen was saying, but his voice sounded different. Steve looked in his direction and saw not the handsome young man he had hung out with on Sunday afternoons, but a half-man-half-beast with glowing eyes and fangs. As he watched the other man was going through some kind of metamorphosis. His jaw grew, extending into a snout. His back was beginning to swell with muscles and arch slightly forward. His normally clean shaven face was sprouting hair all over. "It's nothing personal, Steve, but on the full moon we've got to hunt.

"But the full moon isn't for three days," Steve blurted, not sure what else to say.

"We need practice," Owen said. "You've got about three minutes to run, and then we will hunt you down and kill you. Enjoy the rest of your life. I do hope that you will make the best of it."

Steve was beginning to panic. His heart was racing and he was losing control of his breathing. He was seconds away from breaking into a blind run. He could feel his muscles beginning to tense, ready to propel him into the darkness. He had no destination in mind, he just suddenly had to be anywhere but here.

"And don't worry, I will take care of your wife and daughter," Owen said, his voice now more of a growl than an actual voice.

The words were like a slap to the face, but they had an effect the other man did not expect. Instead of throwing Steve over the edge into a blind panic as Owen had intended, the overt threat towards his daughter had flipped a switch somewhere inside of him. Panic became anger. His sharpened senses came back to him. Suddenly, instead of thinking about running, he was thinking about surviving. In a matter of seconds his mind was going back over the forest he had known his entire life, looking for an escape plan.

"Two minutes," the creature growled.

When Steve did run, he knew where he was going. He headed straight for the mouth of an old deer trail that had wound it's way through these woods for decades. The trail would lead straight to the creek and then on to the backyard of his parents old house. The house had set abandoned since his father had passed away, but he had never been able to bring himself to haul anything out. Everything his parents had owned was still inside, including his father's vast assortment of hunting rifles and pistols. All he had to do was beat those things through the forest.

He burst through the mouth of the trail and into the trees. The bright moonlight didn't reach more than a few feet beyond that point, but he didn't slow down. He had followed this same trail a million times in his life and knew when to turn. It wasn't long before he could hear the sound of the water rushing through the creek, and that made him press even harder.

Behind him the forest erupted with a series of monstrous howls, which he assumed meant those things were after him. Some part of him had already identified them as werewolves, but he still wasn't quite ready to acknowledge that fact yet. But whatever they were, he could hear them as they burst through the trees, crashing through limbs and dead leaves quickly and furiously. As he ran he judged the distance, and he knew he didn't have enough time. They would catch him before he reached the house.

An old gnarled hickory tree had grown along the banks of the creek since his grandfather was a boy. During the rainy season the gentle flowing creek turned into a muddy, rushing river. Over time the rough water had eaten away at the bank around the tree, leaving an opening big enough for a man to hide in. When he was a boy he had hidden there on several occasions to escape a beating from his older brother, Rick. It would mean getting wet, but that was not necessarily a bad thing. Dogs couldn't track well in water, maybe these things had the same problem.

When he knew he was close, Steve took a hard right off of the deer trail and ran straight at the creek bank. He could barely tell where he was, but his memory of the forest proved true. At just the right moment he dove, cleared the steep bank and came crashing down in knee deep water. He could hear at least one of the things closing in quickly, and let himself sink up to his neck in the cold water. Something slithered passed his cheek, but he put it out of his mind. Snakes, even poisonous water snakes, were no match for what was on his trail. He slowly paddled his way towards where he knew the old hickory tree was supposed to be.

A giant black form burst through the trees, clearing the creek and landing on the opposite bank. Before it had gone a dozen feet it stopped. Even over the sound of the water he could hear it sniffing the air, trying to find his trail. It raised it's face towards the sky and howled. Two answers came, one from each side of him. He pressed harder for the safety of the tree roots.

The first creature doubled back, walking the bank of the creek and sniffing the air. Sooner or later it would spot him. To make matters worse, he could hear the approaching crash of the thing's companions.

He reached out for the hickory tree but his hand

found only muddy creek bank. Once again panic threatened to overtake him, but Steve focused on what Owen had said about Miranda and pressed on. A moment later his hand came to rest on the tree's massive root system. He grabbed a root and pulled himself into their midst just as another of the creatures appeared out of the darkness.

The three creatures had moved up and down the creek bank trying to pick up his scent. Then they split up, two heading down stream and the third heading up. He knew then that his idea about the water had been correct. They couldn't smell him in the water, so they assumed he'd tried to escape through it. He slowly counted off two minutes and listened as their sound faded away. He wouldn't allow himself to hope that they would just move on, sooner or later they would come back to where they had started. When they did they would find him.

When he thought it safe enough, Steve moved out of the tree roots and swam to the opposite shore. He carefully climbed the steep, muddy bank and then stood and listened. He heard a howl somewhere downstream, which was answered by another far upstream. They were a good distance away, further than he would have thought. For the first time survival actually seemed possible. He broke into a run, heading straight for his childhood home. His hand was once again playing with the cross around his neck.

Steve broke through the trees, back into the moonlight. He could see the house, not twenty yards away and smiled. Suddenly something huge struck him from the side, lifting him off his feet. As they flew through the air he could feel the creature's coarse fur and hot breath against his cheek. He realized his mistake, now that it was too late. These things might look like animals, but they thought like men.

13

They hit the ground hard and the creature rolled off of him.

Steve tried to regain his footing, but the thing was too fast. It lunged at him.

Instinctively he threw his hands out in front of him. In the brief second before the creature drove its weight into him, Steve realized that he was clutching something in his hand. When the thing had hit him the first time he had been holding onto the cross. The blow had ripped it off of his neck, but somehow he had managed to cling to it.

A massive mouth full of teeth clamped down on his shoulder. With all of his strength he drove the cross into the creature's eye. The teeth let go of him, and the thing made a sound that was somewhere between a cry of anger and a scream of pain. It dropped back, clawing at it's face. In the moonlight Steve could see the broken silver chain attached to the cross dangling across the creature's face.

He ran. Steve crossed the distance to the house, oblivious to the bleeding wound in his shoulder. He didn't bother to unlock the house, he just drove that same shoulder into the old wooden back door. As it exploded inward, his momentum carried him into the back hall. Steve didn't hesitate, he ran straight to his fathers room in the darkness and wrenched the drawer out of the night stand, dumping it out across the dusty comforter on the bed.

He had just enough time to pick up his father's matching Colt .45s before one of the creatures crashed through the bedroom window.

Steve fired both guns into it's chest. The blow might not have killed the creature, but the sudden, unexpected force threw it back through the shattered window.

A second creature was in the hallway. He turned and fired twice. One bullet struck the thing in the face, the other hit it in the throat. It howled in anger and dropped back.

He could hear the two in the yard, pacing around the house, regrouping for another attack. Steve dropped to the ground and pulled an old wooden crate out from under the bed. As always his father had not latched the padlock. He threw the lock off and tore the lid open. The smell of gun oil filled the air and he allowed himself another smile. For the first time in his life he thanked God that his father had been a gun nut. He shoved the pistols into the waistband of his pants and pulled out his father's SKS. 7.62 converted to fully automatic, thanks to conversion kit his father had picked up at some gun show somewhere, and equipped with a fully loaded 55 round clip. He also saw his father's emergency fund-a roll of cash he kept for the day the stock market crashed and all of the banks closed. He shoved the money into the pocket of his jeans.

One of the creatures tried the window again and Steve released a volley of shots that tore through the side of the house. He couldn't tell if he'd hit the thing, but he heard a pained yelp as it dropped back out of site. One of the others released an angry howl.

Steve tossed his father's twelve gauge on the bed and headed for the window. He could see all three of the creatures now standing in the center of the lawn, and for the first time he got a good look at them. Moonlight glinted off the silver chain that still dangled from the smallest creature's eye. That one was jet black. The other two were larger than the first, but it was clear which was the alpha male. They kept looking towards it as if waiting for a command. One of them was gray, the other either a light brown or muddy red.

15

He raised the SKS, took aim at the center of the small pack and opened fire.

He emptied the clip into them, drawing more yelps of pain and angry growls. The bullets did not seem to do any permanent, lasting damage, but the pain seemed to be enough. They drew back into the forest.

Steve watched after them for some time. They hadn't left, they waited in the shadows and watched. Every now and then he would see the glint of red eye shine or hear the sound of one of them moving through the leaves.

Quickly he made his way back to his father's arsenal and started reloading the SKS clip, but it was slow work. Fifty-five rounds was a lot of ammunition. He was up to forty when he heard the creatures approaching again. He tried to get the clip back into the rifle, but they were on him before he had the chance.

The first creature smashed not through the window, but through the actual wall of the house. It was the grey one, and from the sound of it's growling it was angry. He could hear the sounds of another creature moving on the roof.

Steve dropped the clip on the bed and grabbed the shotgun. As the creature made a dive towards him he fired. The twelve guage caught the creature under the chin at almost point blank range, tossing it backwards. It stumbled and fell back through the hole in the wall.

At once he grabbed up the SKS clip and slammed it into the rifle. The second creature came crashing through the ceiling, landing right on top of him. He fell back with the barrel of the gun raised. Gravity and weight impaled the creature on the barrel of the gun. Steve pulled the trigger, emptying forty rounds into the thing's chest cavity from the inside.

It rolled off of him, wrenching the gun from his

hands. The SKS fell to the floor as the creature stumbled for the hole in the wall. Blood was pouring out of it's body like water, leaving a wet trail behind it.

Steve didn't hesitate, he raised the shot gun, pumped in another shell and fired. The blast struck the creature in the center of the back from only a few feet away, blowing a fist sized hole in it's body. He fired again, hitting it in the lower back. It went to it's knees and let out a very human scream of pain.

He pumped in another shell and fired, this time hitting it in the back of the head. Chunks of it's skull blew off, revealing what was underneath.

Steve's hands were shaking as he tried to remember how many times he had fired. He reached into the box beside the bed and grabbed a handful of shotgun shells. Quickly he started reloading.

The black creature suddenly appeared in the opening in front of the red wolf. It raised one massive claw and ripped the other creatures throat out. Then it raised its face towards the sky and howled.

Chapter Two

When Steve opened his eyes, daylight was shining in through the giant hole in the wall. He pressed his palm to his forehead, trying to clear away the fog of the night before. It all seemed like a dream, yet he was staring at the carnage to his father's house. He sat up in the bed and confirmed that the naked corpse of a bearded man still lay just inside the opening. The man's body was riddled with bullet wounds.

He collapsed back on the mattress and looked up at the blue sky now visible through the hole in the ceiling. He felt like he could lay there forever. He was light headed and felt as if he had been drugged.

Steve almost drifted back off to sleep, but a thought came rushing back to him. Owen had threatened Chloe and Miranda. He sat straight up in bed and dropped his heavy feet to the floor. He stuffed the Colt .45s into his jeans and grabbed a speed loader out of the ammo box. He had used just about all of the SKS rounds, so the assault rifle would be useless to him. He knew his father had another stash somewhere around heer, but he didn't have time to look for it. Instead he grabbed a box of shells for the shotgun.

Not wanting to get near the dead man, he turned and headed out the door and down the hall. Steve paused when he caught a glimpse of himself in the mirror. He did not look good at all. He was pale, and his right shoulder was covered in dried blood. He reached up to touch it, expecting a shock of pain, but it never came. Below the dried streaks of blood the skin had healed. He could still see the faint impressions of the teeth that had bitten him, but the wounds were all but gone.

He didn't have time to dwell on it. Steve grabbed the keys to his fathers old Ford and left through the front door, the shotgun laying cold against his bloodied shoul-

19

der. The truck hadn't been started in two years, but he knew it would run. It always had. His father had been one heck of a mechanic, and the old stick shift pickup was parked under a carport at the top of a steep hill. It would work.

Memories of his father threatened to flood his mind as he opened the door, but he pushed them away. Now was not the time for reminiscing. The old pale green and white truck sat in it's usual spot. Dust had collected on the windshield.

He laid the shotgun across the seat. The stale smell of his dad's Old Spice burned his nose. He tried the key, but after two years the battery was dead, so he shifted the truck into neutral and started pushing.

It took no effort to get the old truck moving, and in the blink of an eye he had hoped in, popped the clutch and got the motor fired up. He spun gravel as he pulled out of the driveway and headed for home.

Steve drove slowly down his street. Owens's 4X4 was parked in the grass, like he'd came home in a hurry. He drove by, comfortable that they wouldn't recognize him in the old truck. There was no sign of trouble at either house, but Steve could feel it in the pit of his stomach. He circled the block and parked in front of the next house down the street. He knew the owners, Bill and Bettey Pullman. They would both be at work already, so they wouldn't notice him or the weapon he was carrying.

He quickly crossed the Pullman's yard and darted between their house and Owen's. Even though he knew it wasn't possible, he could hear voices coming from inside the house. Very distinctly he could hear Owen and another man talking, while Chloe pleaded with them and Miranda cried. A wave of hatred like nothing he had ever felt washed over him.

Steve moved quickly around to the front porch and crept quietly up the stairs. Owen's front door was mostly glass, and through it he could see his neighbor and a large bearded man deep in a heated conversation near the back of the house. Chloe lay in the floor, her hands and feet bound. She was stripped down to her bra and panties, and someone had put a dog collar around her neck. He could not see Miranda. Owen had a bandage wrapped around his head and over one of his eyes. He was leaned back in a chair, a drink in his hand.

He checked the shotgun. It had five in the chamber and one in the barrel. He had another handful of shells in his pocket.

"Leave him, he'll die anyway," the bearded man said. "The full moon is in three days."

"People will surprise you, Dave," Owen replied.

"No werewolf will survive his first full moon without a pack to guide him," the one known as Dave argued. "He'll lose his mind to the change, go on a killing spree and then burn out. If the madness doesn't kill him, he'll put a bullet in himself."

"Steve has surprised us already."

"Nobody survives the first full moon alone."

"The Moon Dog."

"Moon Dog?" Dave asked. "You're crazy, that's just a myth you alphas tell to keep us in line."

"I've seen his work," Owen said. "It was back when I was still a lieutenant in my old pack. One of our betas was from a little town in the Moon Dog's territory. He thought he could slip in and out. Just drop by and visit his mom, you know?"

"Really?"

"Yes, really," Owen insisted. "But that old wolf keeps close watch over his bayou. He is aware of everyone and everything that comes in and out. The beta, this kid not much older than eighteen or nineteen gets right up to his mom's driveway. Steps out of the truck and gets torn to shreds. We got pieces of him back in the mail, along with a letter telling us to stay out of Mississippi."

"Your alpha let that go?"

"Orders from on high," Owen said.

"The council?" the other asked.

Owen was about to respond, but stopped. He sniffed the air, and a toothy grin spread across his face.

"Our buddy Steve is close," Owen said.

"Steve!" Chloe cried.

"Shut up!" the bearded man suddenly yelled and kicked her in the ribs.

Steve didn't think, the anger had taken control of him. With the shotgun in front of him he crashed straight through the glass. With unbelievable quickness the bearded man charged straight through the house at him. When they were only a few feet apart Steve fired. The blast caught the man right in the chest, flipping him over backwards.

Momentum carried him forward, past Dave and into the room with Owen and Chloe. He pumped another shell into the barrel and fired. Pellet's sprayed across the other man's left arm, but he didn't even flinch. Chloe cried out to him, but Steve was busy pumping another shell into the gun.

Dave kicked out with his feet, striking Steve in the back of the knee. He pitched forward into Owen, who grabbed frantically at the shotgun. Steve brought it up hard, striking the younger man in the chin and momentarily dazing him. Before he could bring the gun up, Dave struck him hard in the back, knocking him to his knees.

The bearded man was drawing back one clawed hand, aiming for the back of Steve's head, but before he could attack Chloe tackled him from the side. They crashed into a glass topped coffee table, which shattered under their weight.

"Enough!" Owen yelled. He stepped forward, a change washing over his face. His good eye momentarily glowed red, and his teeth seemed to sharpen. "I've had enough of your antics."

Steve could not help himself. There was a unmistakable authority in the other man's voice, and he found himself unable to resist. He tried to raise the gun, but his arms wouldn't move. He felt his knees go weak and sunk to the floor. The gun fell in front of him.

"Do you have any idea the kind of trouble you have caused me?" Owen asked. "You were supposed to be an easy target. You were supposed to get eaten, and then we were going to come back here and make your little wife a member of our pack. No problem. Just another day!"

Steve's eyes cut to Chloe, who was looking up at him with tears in her eyes. He looked back at Owen, who had taken on his human facade again.

"Instead, you put out my eye and kill Charles. Seriously? This has turned into a mess. We can't stay here! The police are going to find his body at what is left of that house, then they'll come here looking for you. When they come to your house, they wont find anybody and will come here. I can't afford to have people looking into my life, Steve, don't you understand that?"

"Screw you," Steve snapped.

He heard the sound of footsteps behind him as the bearded man reappeared. His wounds were already healed. Drying blood soaked the front of his t-shirt.

23

"At least we don't have to look for him now," the other man said.

"True," Owen said. "Let's kill them and go."

"Come on, boss, at least lets get some payback for Charles. Make him suffer a little before you kill him."

Owen smiled thoughtfully. He knelt down next to Chloe and ran a hand through her hair. She shyed away from him and he laughed.

"Keep your hands off of my wife."

"She's mine now, Steve-O," Owen said with a grin. "She'll do anything and everything I tell her to do. I could make her rip your throat out right now and there is nothing you could do to stop it."

"Steve, I would never-"

"Kill him," Owen ordered.

In the blink of an eye Chloe changed. Her eyes burned an amber color and sharp fangs appeared in her mouth. Hair sprang out all up and down her arms. Her manicured fingernails sprouted into sharp, animal-like claws. She struggled against the ropes binding her hands and feet, snapping them. Owen jumped off of her and she bound at Steve, fangs and claws flying.

"Stop," Owen commanded an instant before her teeth would have sank into his throat. Instantly she obeyed. He looked at Steve and grinned. "See, she belongs to me now. Well, me and the rest of my pack. I'm not greedy. I'll share her with them."

"You are a dead man," Steve said. He looked at Chloe. "I swear I'll get you out of this."

Chloe snarled at him through her fangs. Owen and the other man laughed.

"Get the girl," Owen said.

The bearded man walked to a closed door and pushed it open. He reached inside and picked Miranda up by her throat. He cries turned to a strangling sound and

24

Steve's hands balled into fists. Unseen by the others, he crawled a step or two closer.

"Well don't kill her yet," Owen told the other man, who set the little girl down at his feet. Miranda saw Steve and tried to run to him, but the ma grabbed her by the collar and held her back. "Maybe we should let Steve kill her himself, huh? How's that for punishment?"

"That would be fun to watch," the other agreed.

"Baby, close your eyes," Steve told his daughter. "Close your eyes tight, and in a few minutes this will all be over."

"Daddy, I'm scared."

"I know baby, but just listen to me," he said. "Close your eyes and think about our trip to the beach."

"And the dolphins?"

"Yes, the dolphins."

"Touching but we really do need to go," Owen said. He looked at the other man and smiled. "I'm thinking maybe we let the wife do it. That way he loses both the women he loves in one bloody attack. I mean, what man could forgive his wife for slaughtering their only child like that?"

"That's rough," the other agreed.

"I would never-"

"Kill her," Owen ordered Chloe.

Chapter Three

"Kill her," Owen ordered, and at once Chloe leapt to her feet. The change overtook her almost instantly. Her small, delicate hands curled into threatening claws. The lower part of her face seemed to stretch into the vague shape of a snout, and her teeth grew pointy and sharp. She snarled mindlessly at Miranda.

"Sit back and watch, Steve-O," Owen laughed.

Steve reacted without thinking. He could almost feel Owen's hold over him as it broke, and every muscle in his body drove him forward. In that moment Chloe was no longer his wife, she was a monster intent on hurting his daughter. In one quick motion he grabbed her by the dog collar and sent her crashing through the window at the back of the house.

Dave lunged at him, but Steve drove his elbow backwards into the man's face. He felt bones crush and the spray of blood.

Owen was starting to get to his feet. Steve swung at him, unaware that his hands had changed into claws until he slashed the man's stomach open.

Owen howled in pain.

Dave had recovered and was starting for him again. Steve scooped the shotgun up and swung it around. He hit the man in the face from only a few feet away. Dave's face was obliterated by the blast. He clawed frantically at himself and collapsed to the floor crying out in pain.

"Stop it now!" Owen ordered. He was holding his stomach in with his hands as he got to his feet, his wounds already starting to heal. "I command you to stop this right now."

"You're not my boss," Steve said. He pumped another shell into the gun and fired. The blast struck Owen in his injured midsection and sent him crashing back into

27

his chair, which flipped over.

"I'll hunt you down and kill you both!"

Steve dropped the gun and picked Miranda up. She was crying but still had her eyes closed tightly. With her clutched to his chest he ran out of the house and across the neighbor's yard. He set her in the passenger's seat of the truck and crawled across.

As he started his father's truck, a flash of movement caught his attention. A large grey werewolf appeared around the corner of the house, running straight at them. As he shifted the truck into gear and pulled away, he saw the dog collar around the beast's neck and sighed. He had saved his daughter, but he had lost his wife.

Steve finally relaxed a little after they reached the edge of town. He knew from experience that the damage he had done to the werewolves was superficial. They would heal quickly, and then they would be on his trail. Time was not on his side. At least he had a little bit of a head start. He had no idea how easily they would be able to track him, but he was pretty sure that even werewolves would be limited by the laws of physics. They could only move as quickly as a vehicle would allow, they weren't, after all, blessed with the ability of flight.

From Miltonboro they headed north on County Road One, which lead into Pine Grove. There was a hardware store called Red's alongside the road where he thought he could get a car seat and some other supplies they might need. They were items that might be cheaper at one of the big box stores, but they could get in and out of Red's faster. Time was the most important thing right now, because he wasn't running for his own life, he was running for Miranda. He would do what it took to keep her safe.

"Where are we going daddy?"

28

"Just taking a little trip, baby."

"To get away from the monsters?"

"Yeah, to get away from the monsters," he said, not knowing how else to answer.

"Mommy is a monster," she said softly. There was neither sadness nor fear in her voice, just a sense of resignation that made Steve's heart break.

"I don't know baby."

"She is, I seed her," Miranda insisted. "She was going to eat me."

"Let's not worry about mommy right now," he said, trying to find something to say that might make it a little better, but coming up with nothing. "We've just got to get somewhere safe, and then we'll worry about mommy."

"Will mommy get better?"

"I really don't know, baby," he admitted. "But if there is anything I can do to make her better, I will."

"And you wont let her eat me?"

"No, I can promise you that," Steve told her. "I will not let mommy or anyone else eat you. Right now keeping you safe is the most important thing in the world to me."

"I love you daddy," she said.

"I love you too."

They drove in silence for the rest of the trip. When buildings began to appear on the outskirts of Pine Grove, Miranda seemed to brighten a little. A trip to town usually meant a new toy, and she, like all children, was always excited about a new toy.

Steve turned the truck into the gravel parking lot of Red's, and Miranda's excitement seemed to dwindle a little.

"Why we going here?"

"We just need to pick up a few things for our

trip," he told her.

Chapter Four

Red's Hardware had been in business for over a hundred years, at least that was what the painted sign that hung on the front of the building promised. Steve knew that it had at least been around since he was Miranda's age. His father had made the trip over to the Grove at least once a month for as long as he could remember, and not because he needed nails. There was a perfectly good hardware store in Miltonboro where he had shopped for all of his hardware needs. He came to Red's for what they specialized in. Guns.

Although the owners called Red's a hardware store, it was really a store that catered to the needs of every self respecting redneck. There was a special NASCAR section in the front, filled with hats, t-shirts and other merchandise from all of the popular drivers. Just beyond that was a section of furniture, mostly either camouflage or hardwood designs. The center of the store was a mix-up of "As Seen on TV" junk, novelty items and various knick knacks that would look good in the same room with a mounted deer head. In the front left of the store was a section that sold baby items, such as cribs, teething rings and car seats.

Steve gave the seats a quick once over, and then grabbed the one that looked the closest to the one in Chloe's car. Miranda playful grabbed at it as he stuffed it down into the cart.

"Can I have a toy, daddy?" she asked, and although he was in a hurry to get back on the road, he agreed. The girl had just seen her mother turn into a werewolf, how could he not buy her a toy?

He pushed the cart down an isle filled with discount toys, mostly cheap rip-offs of the name brand items you'd find at the big box stores. Her attention automatically drifted to the princess dolls. She looked them over,

31

absently biting her lower lip the same way her mother always had when she had to make a tough decision.

"No, I want a doggy," she said at last, pointing to a row of stuffed animals.

"Are you sure?"

"Aww, that doggy is cute," she cried, pointing at a large German Shepherd. He handed it too her and she hugged it against her chest like it was the greatest gift she'd ever received.

Steve started pushing the cart again, not even realizing that he was heading towards the back of the store.

"What are you going to name him?" he asked.

"I'm going to call him....dadda!" she said with a laugh.

For a moment he felt sick to his stomach. Miranda had already lost her mother, and as far as he was concerned, she would soon be losing her father as well. It wasn't fair. She was still so little. She didn't deserve to lose the only life she had ever known. But she would never be safe with him. He was going to have to leave her somewhere.

That was when he thought of his brother Rick for the first time. They rarely talked. Oh, they exchanged the obligatory Christmas card, and usually called each other on their birthdays, but that was it. Except for their father's funeral, they hadn't gotten together as a family since their mother died. Now it looked like they never would. But he and Rick had a history of being there for each other, even when they were teenagers who seemingly hated each other. No one messed with a Slate. They took care of their own, even when they didn't want to.

"Hey baby, you want to meet your Uncle Rick?"

"I know Uncle Rick," Miranda said. "He came to see pap-pap at the bad church."

He smiled. Bad church had been what she had called the funeral home where they'd had her grandfather's services.

"How would you like to go to his house?"

"Right now?"

"Well, yes, we can leave right now but it will take us a while to get there," he said.

"Sure," she replied. "Does he have a dog? I really like doggies."

Detective Tad Tuttle of the Miltonboro Police Department parked his unmarked cruiser at the bottom of the hill and sighed, looking up at the collection of emergency vehicles that blocked the driveway. Tuttle was a big man, standing nearly six four and weighing a little over three hundred pounds. He was overweight, but not what would be considered fat. He was just a big man. His size had just made it that much worse that people had called him "Tiny" up until the day he was promoted to Detective. They still called him that, now they just did it out of his presence.

He climbed out of his cruiser and stood looking at the old house on the hill, cursing his luck that it hadn't been located another half dozen feet down Duke Drive. Then it would have been outside the city limits and out of his jurisdiction. He hated dead bodies, and he'd served long enough to see more than his fair share. This little town had a dark history.

"Morning Tad," said one of the EMTs who had wandered down the hill for a smoke.

"What we got, Jimmy?" Tad asked, straightening his suit.

"I don't know what to tell you," the man said. "Nothing for me, I can tell you that. The place is a wreck."

Tad nodded and started up the hill. A few uniformed officers were milling around the driveway, clearly waiting for him to take control of the scene. He didn't know any of them by name because not a one of them was actually from Miltonboro. Actually, Tad was one of a select few locals on the force. Most of the local guys were either working in the mine or cooking meth. At least that was how it seemed to him most of the time.

County Coroner Todd Maxwell met him at the top of the hill. Like most elected officials in the county, Max was a legacy. Not only had his family owned Maxwell's Funeral Home for more than a hundred years, each generation had also served as the coroner. Death was their family business.

"What do we have, Max?"

"Not much, I am afraid," the other man said. Todd Maxwell looked like one of Santa's elves standing next to Tad. He was rail thin and just over five foot four. "It's out of my area of expertise, but I'd say someone fired off a few thousand rounds inside that place. Not really that surprising, I knew Harold Slate. We went way back. Last time I was in that house he was armed better than the 101st Airborne. Handguns, shotguns and rifles. I think I even saw an AK-47 inside."

He was well aware that in addition to his funeral and corner jobs, Max was also on the board of directors of the Fletcher County Gun Club. He and Tad shot together just about every weekend. He seemed to remember seeing Harold Slate at the club several times through the years, usually with a different gun each time.

"I played baseball with Steve Slate," Tad said.

"Yeah, that was his youngest boy," Max told him. "He still lives in town, as far as I know. There was an older boy, but he moved away years ago.

"I haven't thought about Steve Slate in at least

34

twenty years," Tad said thoughtfully. "So what's going on? We got a body?"

"If you asked me, I'd say that someone died in there," Max said. "Whole lot of blood. I mean a whole lot. But as for a body, we got nothing."

"Lot of blood, no body," Tad said. "Enough for you to say we've got a dead body?"

"I'd feel confident to sign off on that, but I can't tell you if it's a human body. Could very well be that a bunch of drunk teenagers shot the place up...maybe killed a deer or two in the process. I did see a lot of hair in there. Probably some kind of animal. I wont know more on the hair or the body until I get something back from the State Police Crime Lab in Madisonville."

"How long?"

"At least a day or two, and that's if I can call in a few favors," Max told him. "I've seen it take six months to get reports back before. But that's been several years ago."

"Well do what you can," he told the coroner, and then walked in through the front door of the house.

The scent of gunpowder still hung in the air.

A half hour away, Steve Slate was pulling his father's old Ford into the Pilot truck stop on the outskirts of town. The place was commonly known as 'The Last Chance', mainly because it was the last chance to buy gas, food or anything else before leaving town. In some weird twist of fate, the seventh largest town in the state had grown up without access to a four lane highway. The main artery that brought goods to and from Pine Grove was Highway 1, a rural stretch of blacktop that ran 28 miles through rural Kentucky countryside. At some point the state had taken over maintenance of the road, redesignated it with a number that none of the locals used and

35

then promised to widen it to four lanes.

Steve had been six the first time the Highway Transportation Cabinet talked about widening the road, but something always got in the way. On more than one occasion it had been lack of funding. One other had been law suits from property owners along the route. He really had his doubts that the road would ever be widened.

Steve parked the truck at the pump and got out. Miranda was sleeping soundly in her seat, the stuffed dog clutched against her chest. An odd sensation passed over him then. It was like a bright spotlight coming on in the middle of the night, except it was midday and there was no bright light. Yet his mind or body was still telling him that it was there.

He turned to his left, looking towards the bank of diesel pumps that lined the side of the truck stop. He knew that was where the sensation was coming from, even if he could not explain what it was. The only truck there at the moment was a long haul rig pulling a trailer for one of the outfits you always see on the highway but never know what they transport. A large man with a red beard was staring back at him, the nozzle still in his hand.

The wind shifted and a new scent hit his nose. He recognized it. He had never smelt it before but knew it anyway. It was the smell of a werewolf. He knew in that second, without a shadow of a doubt, that the man watching him was a werewolf. It triggered a moment of panic inside him, and he almost got back into his dad's truck and left.

What stopped him was the sight of his daughter sleeping in her car seat. He had no idea if this newcomer was a threat, but he knew Owen was. He knew Owen, Dave and Chloe would be on his trail by now, intent on tracking him down and slaughtering his sleeping daughter. Anger replaced the panic and he swiped his card at the pump. They needed to get on the road fast, and the only way to do that was by filling up the truck's gas tank.

He and the trucker watched each other while they pumped their fuel. It occurred to Steve that he really knew nothing about the creature that he was becoming, other than what Hollywood had to say. In the movies werewolves were always vicious outcasts, usually in leather and jack boots. They had no need for civilization, their only desire was to hunt and kill humans, just as Owen had intended to do with him.

Was that all there was? Once the full moon took him, was that what he would become? Just another mindless killing machine? He refused to believe that. He had seen what it had done to Chloe, but he has resisted. He had to believe that he could salvage some kind of life out of this.

Finally the trucker raised a hand in salute and climbed into the cab of his truck. He turned out of the parking lot and headed into town. Steve breathed a sigh of relief.

A Pine Grove Police cruiser turned into the truck stop, but he paid it no attention.

"I really wish I knew what happened here," Tad Tuttle said to one of the uniformed officers who was assisting him. The guy's name was Daren, and all Tad knew about him was that the guy loved the St. Louis Cardinals. It was all he talked about. "Okay, we need to track down the property owner. Max said a guy named Steve Slate is the current owner, but he doesn't live here. He does still live in town though. Get out an APB on him and have someone check his house."

"Steve Slate, got it," Daren said. He nodded and

37

stood looking around the scene. Crime scene?

Tad still wasn't sure, but he knew something had gone down here. He glared at the cop who still hadn't moved and asked, "Are you going to call it in, or are you going to stand here staring at me?"

"Oh, sorry sir, on my way to call it in."

When the other man was gone, Tad tried to remember everything he could about Steve Slate, which wasn't much. Steve had played baseball but had never been one of the jocks. Outside of games and practice, Tad and his friends never hung out with Slate. Slate never came to any of the team parties. Since high school he had seen the man even less, if he'd seen him at all.

His gut told him that Steve Slate was involved in whatever had happened here. Either he had shot someone or had been shot himself, and then the shooter had disposed of the body.

He sniffed the gun powder that still hung on the air and looked around at the spent shell casings. You didn't use that kind of firepower to kill one man. Something was wrong here, he just didn't know what.

Tad stepped over to the gapping hole in the wall and looked out at the grass, which didn't look to have been mowed in some time. He could still see where someone or something had trampled it, making circles around the house. He looked down and saw what looked like a very large dog print in the dirt.

Chapter Five

Patrolman Clint Board had his coffee in hand and was heading back to finish his shift when he saw the old Ford F-150 filling up at the pumps. Something about the truck triggered an alarm in his head. He looked it over slowly as he headed back to his cruiser. At last it dawned on him. The tags on the back were expired. He smiled, satisfied with himself. He opened the door and set his coffee in the cup holder. He started to call it in but decided he'd chat to the driver first. He wasn't a heartless man. Sometimes people renewed their tags and just forgot to put them on the vehicle. He hated to call it in, because once the ball started rolling he'd have to write the guy up.

He straightened his uniform and unsnapped the top of his holster out of habit. The driver of the pickup wasn't watching him, he was watching a semi that was pulling out on the highway and heading east. The man didn't look like a threat. He was a smallish man dressed in a Carhartt t-shirt and jeans. He didn't appear to be jumpy or agitated, only concerned with the truck that had just driven away,

Maybe he used to be a truck driver, Clint thought, but that didn't seem right. He didn't seem tough enough to be a trucker.

He was three feet away from the back of the pickup when he heard a loud crash from behind him. Clint drew his gun and spun around. One of the cashiers had a teenage boy by the collar and was holding him against the front of the propane storage case. A knife lay on the ground at the boy's feet, and the cashier was slamming him into the metal case again and again.

"You come to my job and try to rob me, punk!" the man was yelling at the kid. Clint wasn't sure if he was imitating Dirty Hairy or if he just sounded that. "I

39

don't think so.."

"Okay now, lets calm down," Board ordered as he moved back to the front of the truck stop. "Hershel, let the kid go."

Hershel let the kid go and took a step back. The kid's eyes went from Clint's face to his gun, and for just a second Clint thought he was going to bolt. Then his face and shoulders sank in defeat.

"What's your name kid?"

"Bobby Durbin," the kid told him.

It took fifteen minutes to get the issue with the kid sorted out. By then Hershel and Bobby Durbin were both apologizing. He let the kid go with a stern warning, don't come back unless you're going to pay. He then warned Hershel about roughing up kids, even if they were stealing bubble gum and candy.

By the time he was finished, the old pickup was gone.

"He's been here," Owen said, sniffing the air.

"Recently," Dave agreed.

The pair moved quickly through Red's Hardware store, following the trail that Steve had left only a few minutes before. Just like the wolves of the animal kingdom, werewolves were blessed with an amazing sense of smell. Picking one of their own out of all the other scents was nothing. Once they were on the open road it would be harder, but the alpha male had faith in his own abilities.

"Where is he headed?" Dave asked. "Seven days and he's just going to change and kill the girl anyway. Why would he run?"

"He's got somewhere to go," Owen growled. "We need to ask the girl, maybe she'll have an idea."

They stepped out of Red's and into the sunlight

as a semi rumbled into the parking lot. Owen sensed it first, but Dave was only a few milliseconds behind. The scent of a werewolf was all over the truck. Both men's eyes suddenly burned orange, and claws sprang out of their finger tips.

The truck went around the side of the building towards the loading dock.

"Get the girl," Owen ordered and started running. If anyone had seen him, they would have had to look twice, because he moved with a speed and grace that no man could possibly possess.

The driver of the truck was ready for him. As Owen approached, he dropped to the ground, already transformed. He took up a defensive stance and growled a warning. Owen matched his growl, unwilling to back down.

"What is the deal with this town?" the truck driver asked. "I've been coming here for thirty years and never seen one werewolf. Today I see two..." That was when Dave and Chloe sprinted around the corner. "Make that four. Why don't you go on your way and let me be, little wolf man?"

"Where was he?" Owen demanded. His teeth were sharpening and his jaw was beginning to protrude.

"Getting out of here, where do you think?" the driver snarled. His shirt began to rip as his muscles twisted and expanded. Dark brown fir protruded from the openings. "I told you to leave me alone. This is neutral ground, you have no claim here."

Owen was a young alpha with a small pack, often leading other packs to try taking advantage of him. The only solution was not to take any pressure from anyone. When pushed he always reacted swiftly and viciously. It might not earn him respect in the eyes of the others, but at least it made them think twice before crossing him.

41

Dave moved to stand side by side with his alpha. Chloe stood a few paces behind, still holding onto her human form for the time being.

"Kill him," Owen ordered.

He and Dave moved as one. Both men seemed to rip out of their human form on the first step, because by the second they were in full werewolf form. The driver laughed, catching the other two by the throat, one in each hand. He slammed them down on the gravel parking lot and then slashed a claw across Dave's chest.

Owen was struggling to his feet, but the driver drove himself forward into his chest. The two werewolves tumbled across the gravel, stirring up a cloud of dust. Teeth gnashed at his throat, and it took every muscle in his body for Owen to hold the larger, more powerful werewolf at bay.

Dave managed to regain his feet and growled at the truck driver. He jumped, intending to go for the other werewolf's jugular, but one massive arm swung up just in time, making him miss his mark. But the blow knocked the other wolf off of Owen.

Chloe was staying as far back from the battle as possible. She wanted to run, to get away while she could, but she had been given her orders. Unlike her husband, she had been unable to overcome the alpha male's orders. He told her not to try and escape, so she simply could not. She was a prisoner without bars.

Owen made a lunge at the driver, who delivered a sudden crushing punch to his chest. He fell to the ground, at least three ribs crushed on his right side. For just a moment his resolve wavered and he started trying to scramble backwards. The other werewolf was grinning as he moved in for the kill.

"Help me," Owen cried in his head. When fully transformed, werewolves have only limited ability to speak, but within a pack the members share a form of telepathy that allows them to work as a group. His message was received.

The truck driver drew back with one clawed hand, ready to take Own's head off. At the last second his chest exploded outwards. One small clawed hand burst through his ribs clutching a still beating heart in it's grasp.

As the werewolf collapsed to the ground at her feet, Chloe raised the heart to her mouth and ate.

After leaving the Pilot station, Steve turned the pickup onto Highway 1 and headed west. Miranda was still asleep. He did his best not to think about what was going on. He had to get his daughter to safety first, then he could worry about everything else. He drove most of the way from Pine Grove to I-69 in autopilot.

Once he hit the interstate they headed south. Miranda woke up somewhere around the town of Hanson, Kentucky. They blew past the exit without a second thought, but a half dozen miles later Miranda saw a sign advertising a number of fast food places.

"Daddy, I want chicken nuggets," she said. "Can we pwease stop?"

Steve looked in the rearview mirror, aware that somewhere behind them was a pack of werewolves intent on killing them. He had no way of knowing where they were. For all he knew they had given up on following him and were headed in a completely different direction. But he didn't really believed that. Even if it wasn't logical, he knew they were chasing them.

"Daddy, pwease," she said, flashing her eyebrows at him. "Pretty pwease."

He couldn't help himself. Miranda was just a little girl, and she hadn't eaten all day. When he saw the

43

exit for Madisonville, he quickly turned off the interstate and followed the signs.

It was going on mid-afternoon but the lines at the various fast food places they passed were hanging on. With little other choice he pulled the truck in line and waited. Every minute they sat there seemed like an eternity. Steve kept checking the mirror and fidgeting with the radio. Sweat was breaking out on his forehead and his heart was racing.

Steve was on the verge of pulling out of line and getting back on the road.

"Why are you sweating daddy?" Miranda asked, and his momentary panic passed.

"I'm hot I guess, baby."

"I'm not hot daddy," she said, giving him a doubtful look. "I think it feels fabulous."

He smiled.

Chapter Six

They got their food and got back on the road without incident. They followed I-69 as it made it's peculiar way across Kentucky, first going south on the former Pennyrile Parkway, then west on the former Western Kentucky Parkway and finally merging with I-24 to head west towards Illinois. Eventually I-69 separated from I-24, but they kept heading west.

It happened just after the two interstates went their own way. A middle aged woman in a black BWM shot by them, then swerved across into his lane, almost hitting the front of Steve's truck. He had always suffered from what Chloe had called 'road rage', but he'd never experienced anything like this. He gritted his teeth and slammed on the gas.

He had always heard people use the phrase 'I saw red', and in that instant he understood. A primal anger bubbled to the surface. Every inch of his body wanted to force the BMW off the road and rip the driver's throat out. He saw it in his head as he closed in on the other vehicle. He could the driver frantically trying to wave an apology as she turned down the exit, but it didn't matter. All that mattered was killing her.

"Is this Uncle Rick's house?" Miranda asked.

The spell wasn't broken, but for just a moment Steve hesitated. He glanced up at the rearview and what he saw there terrified him. His eyes were glowing a burnt orange color, and he had an evil grin spread across his face. If he had just been grinning at the idea of murdering someone it would have bothered him, but what really caught him was his teeth. They were no longer the teeth he was used to seeing in the mirror, they had grown into sharp, pointed fangs.

Steve slammed on the brakes and pulled the truck to the shoulder of the exit. The BMW sped away, but he no longer cared. He was trying to control the red cloud that was trying to creep over his body, quickening his breathing and causing the hair on his arm to stand on end. He threw open his door and jumped out into the road, nearly stumbling when his feet hit asphalt.

He could feel the wolf trying to struggle to the surface, trying to push him inside so it could get out and run wild. For a moment the change had gone so far that he could feel what it felt. Steve suddenly knew the feeling of being an animal locked inside a cage. Freedom was just seconds away and it excited and terrified him at the same time.

Steve looked down at his hands and wasn't surprised to see that they were changing into claws. He made a fist, squeezing them into his palm hard enough to draw blood. He remembered hearing in some horror movie where the werewolf had said pain helped him maintain control, but that was a lie. The creature trapped inside him was a monster with a primal nature. It did not fear pain. Pain infuriated it.

At the last moment, just when he could feel the wolf about to seize control, the thought of Miranda stopped him. If he changed, what would happen to her? At worst he would kill her himself, but if, somehow, he managed to get away from her, she would be a three year old girl abandoned on the side of the road. Anybody could come along and take her.

He focused on her, and for the first time he became aware of her crying in the truck, calling to him. Steve didn't dare turn. He didn't want her to see his face as it was now. She'd already seen her mother turn into a monster, he would not have her see him do the same thing.

He breathed.

"Da-a-a-addy-y-y-y!" she cried.

He closed his eyes and focused on controlling his breathing.

"Daddy come back!"

Steve could feel the wolf going. It didn't go all the way, but it was under control again. He was back to himself. He stood a moment longer, willing himself to be normal again, at least in appearance. When he felt that he was back, he forced a smile and turned back to the truck.

"I'm right here baby," he said.

Tad Tuttle stood in the middle of the Slate's living room and wished that he still smoked. Or drank. The little suburban house wasn't as much of a wreck as the old farmhouse had been, but it was pretty well trashed. The back door had been knocked clear off it's hinges. The television lay face down on the floor. Blood had dried in a pool on the white carpet near the shattered back door.

"Looks like we've got a problem," he told the patrolman standing behind him. "Both of the Slate's vehicles are home, so they didn't leave in their own vehicles. We need to find out if they had access to anything else. Maybe the father had a vehicle."

Owen was driving down I-24 at ninety when he felt a wave of energy so strong that it nearly made him black out. He managed to hold on, but the truck momentarily swerved over onto the rumble strips. The sudden growling sound beneath the tires woke Dave, who had been dozing in the passenger seat.

"Did you feel that?" Owen asked in awe as he got the truck back under control.

"Feel what?"

"Steve," Owen told him. "He just changed. Or at least he almost did. I felt him fight it off."

47

"You felt that?" Dave asked.

"I made him," Owen explained. "There is...always will be...a connection between us. Not really like a mental connection, I can't read his mind or anything, but I can feel what he's feeling."

"Can you feel what I'm feeling?" the other man asked and then yawned.

"Screw you Dave," Owen said with a snarl. "This is big. He shouldn't be able to do that. He's too young. When the change grabs him he shouldn't be able to fight it off like that. I know older wolves who have trouble doing that."

"He shouldn't have been able to fight you off either," a soft voice said from the back seat. "But he did."

"Don't tempt me," he snapped at the newest member of his pack. Chloe was laying in the back floorboard, an old blanket wrapped tightly around her. "I'm only keeping you alive because you're good to look at, and because I want to use you to punish him."

"He'll kill you."

"That's funny," Owen said. "He can't. Maybe if I keep him around long enough he could challenge me, but he's too young. I could beat him with one hand tied behind my back."

"How about one eye?"

Owen glared at her in the rearview mirror. He had removed the eye patch, but he still hadn't regained much sight in his bad eye. All he could see was a rainbow of dancing colors. In another day or two he should be whole again. Surely no later than the full moon he would be whole. Until then he had to deal with limited vision and an eye that was a mixture of black and red.

"Shut up," he ordered, and she listened. "You need to try and be a little more like Charles, before you end up just like him."

48

In the rear view he saw her look towards the corpse stuffed into the back floorboard and grimace. He laughed but started thinking it might be a good time to get rid of the body. They removed it from the old farmhouse in hopes that the absence of a body might at least slow the authorities down, but it was starting to stink.

"What is going on in this town?" Tad asked. He had walked out of the Slate's back door to take a look in the yard, and that was when he got a look at the house next door. The back window had been shattered, and shards of broken glass littered the back grass.

"Hey Darren, find out who lives there," he told the patrolman. Before the man could grab his mic Tad turned to look at the house again.

"On it, sir," the other man said.

Tad walked across the Slate's yard far enough that he could see into the neighbor's driveway. He didn't see a vehicle. He started running scenarios in his head, and none of them were good. They all ended with one or all of the Slate's dead.

"Dispatch said that the neighbor is a guy named Owen Black, he just moved here from Texas a few months ago," Darren said. "Oh, and Harold Slate had a late 72 Ford F-150. Tags and registration are out, but the title is still in his name."

"Does Owen Black have a vehicle?"

"2013 Chevy Silverado Z-71."

"Put out a BOLO on both trucks," he ordered. "One of them has or did have a dead body in it."

He crossed the rest of the way into Black's back yard, approaching the broken window. The grass around the house had a trampled look to it, and he thought of the print he'd seen at the farm house. Tad dropped to one knee and studied the ground. There it was again. A dog

49

print easily the size of his hand.

Chapter Seven

Just before dark they passed a sign that told him the town of Wickliffe was only five miles ahead. Beyond that would be the Mississippi River then Missouri. If he drove all night, he could be at Rick's by bed time. He breathed a sigh of relief, and his father's truck picked that moment to quit on him. The engine sputtered, popped and then seemed to explode. Smoke poured from the vents, from the hood and out the exhaust. A dark brown, almost black liquid sprayed across the bottom of the windshield.

Steve guided the truck to the shoulder, where it finally gave up the ghost. In her car seat Miranda was clutching her puppy and crying again. He knew how she felt.

"Well, it looks like the truck just broke down," he told his daughter.

"Daddy, can you fix it?" she whined.

"Daddy can look, but he's not really much of a mechanic, baby," Steve told her. He looked in the rear-view mirror and could almost feel his pursuers closing in. He grabbed the shotgun from behind the seat and stepped out onto the road. "I'll be right back."

Steve had never taken any automotive classes in high school and had barely listened when his father had tried to teach him how to do the work for himself. His belief had always been that it was better to pay an expert that to mess it up himself. Suddenly he was reconsidering that decision.

He popped the hood and was greeted by a breath that tasted like burnt rubber and oil. As the cloud of smoke cleared, he could see that everything under the hood was in fact coated in oil. The truck wasn't going anywhere tonight, of that much he was sure.

A pair of headlights appeared on the horizon and

a strange feeling hit him in the pit of his stomach. Even before he could smell them, he could sense them. They had found him and he had nowhere to run. He got Miranda out of her car seat and told her to stay behind him. He double checked to be sure the gun was fully loaded, then stepped to the back of the truck.

Owen's pickup pulled to the shoulder and both of the front doors burst open. Steve raised the shotgun and blew out the front driver's side headlight, causing both of the other werewolves to take a step back.

"Enough with the guns already," Owen said. "You know you can't kill us with a shotgun. You'll just make us angry."

"How's the eye?"

"I'm gonna...." Owen began, but trailed off. He bit his lip as if thinking about something. "I felt it when you almost changed earlier. It took a lot of strength to hold that back. I could really use someone like you in my pack, after all, we are a man short now."

"So after everything else, now you want to let me live?" Steve asked, doubtfully.

"Look, we're a little pack," Owen said. "There is strength in numbers, and right now we don't have the numbers. Lets just leave it all in the past. You can come with us, and you can have your wife back."

"Chloe's okay?"

"Of course she is okay. Girl, get out here."

The back driver's side door opened and his wife climbed out. She was wearing Daisy Duke cutoffs and a tight t-shirt. Her hair was a mess. He had never seen her dressed as slutty, and it surprised him that it was a good look for her.

"Mommy!" Miranda called out.

"Hey honey, mommy loves you."

Miranda tried to pull away from him, but Steve

held her back.

"So you mean to let me and my family live, if we agree to follow you?" he asked.

"Well, you and your wife," Owen said. "The little girl, now that's a different story. We don't have a place for a baby. I'll let Dave take care of her if it makes you feel better."

"You will not touch a hair on her head," Steve growled, surprised by the force that came out of him. It was enough to make Dave and Chloe take a step back, bewildered.

"On second thought, I think if I let you live you're just going to end up trying to killing me anyway," Owen told him. "Let's kill them and get back on the road."

Tad Tuttle was on his way into Pine Grove to talk to a friend on the local police department when he saw the lights at Red's Hardware. He whipped into the parking lot and pulled around to where the other law enforcement vehicles were parked.

A patrol officer approached as he climbed out of his car. Tad flipped his suit coat open to reveal the badge clipped to his belt, which seemed to be enough for the patrolman.

"Who is in charge here?"

"Captain Mackey!" he called to a balding man in a police uniform.

Captain Mackey was the image of a Hollywood police captain, short and stalk with quickly receding white hair. He wasn't smoking a cigarette, but a pack could easily be seen in the breast pocket of his uniform. He gave Tad a quick once over and nodded.

"Captain Mack Mackey," he said, his voice graveled by years of smoking.

"Detective Tad Tuttle, Miltonboro PD," Tad said.

"I was on my way over to confer with Detective Rollins on a case I'm working."

"Yeah, I saw the bulletin earlier," Mackey told him. "Think your suspect came this way?"

"Could be, but mostly I'm grasping at straws," he admitted. "If I was going to leave Miltonboro in a hurry, this is the way I'd come. So what do you have here?"

"Dead truck driver," the captain said. He glanced at his notebook, checking the victim's name. "Wayne Shelley. Night shift cashier found him on her way into work. Looks like he had his hear ripped right out of his chest."

"Gruesome."

Both men paused and looked at the bloody patch of dirt and gravel where the dead body had been.

"Very," said Mackey. "I'm at a loss to tell you how it happened. Maybe the ME can give us something to work with."

"Any security cameras out here?" asked Tad.

"Nah, the gun nuts that frequent this place aren't too big on surveillance. There is a bank across the road, we might be able to see the parking lot out front on it, but it wont show us what happened."

"Any chance I can watch it with you? Might see if any of the folks I'm looking for show up."

"Your buddy Rollins is over there now waiting on the bank president. If he don't care, then knock yourself out."

Tad started to walk away, but stopped and looked down at the spot where Wayne Shelley had died. He didn't see any animal tracks, but there was enough gravel on the lot that they still could have been there.

"Any sign of animal tracks, or animal bite marks on the body?" Tad asked. The captain gave him a surprised look. "There were weren't there?"

"No tracks or bite marks, but there was animal fir around the wound," Mackey told him. "Guess this might be tied to your case after all, huh?"

Steve couldn't believe they were going to attack on the side of the road. It wasn't as if they were on the side of a busy interstate, but US 60 wasn't exactly an isolated country road. Every few seconds a vehicle zipped by. He lifted Miranda into his arms and stepped back towards the driver's door.

"You know that wont do any good," Owen warned. "Why don't you just come over here and man up?"

Steve searched his wife's faces. She was still in there, he could tell. Chloe was crying. If he could get Miranda to safety, and then survive the coming full moon, he would try to save her too.

Owen took a step forward and Steve fired.

Trooper Sebastian Kyle was just about to get off duty when a BOLO came across the screen of his in car computer. The authorities in some place called Miltonboro were searching suspects in a possible homicide. The descriptions and license number of an older Ford pickup and a new Chevy Silverado appeared on the screen, along with the license numbers. He scanned them but didn't really expect to need the information.

It was just starting to get dark when he came up on two vehicles parked on the side of the road, only about five minutes after the BOLO crossed his screen. His mind was elsewhere and his shift had been over for five minutes. He would have passed them without a second thought if the sudden flash of a shotgun muzzle hadn't broken him from his thoughts. He slammed on his breaks and slid to a stop in the middle of the road, almost

55

directly beside the Chevy.

Regulation required him to don his hat upon leaving the vehicle, but he didn't even think about it. Kyle had his 10mm service weapon in his hand by the time his boots hit the asphalt. His training kicked in instantly, identifying three suspects near the newer truck, and a fourth man and small child near the older one. That was the one holding the weapon.

"Drop the gun," he barked as he took aim over the roof of the car.

All eyes were suddenly on him. A quick assessment told him that the three people nearest him were either not armed, or they at least weren't holding any weapons. The man with the gun was his first priority.

"Officer, you don't understand," the man with the gun said. "These people are trying to hurt my daughter."

"That might be, sir, but first thing we have to do is put the shotgun down," Kyle said with authority. "We'll sort the rest of it out afterwards."

It was then that the BOLO came back to him. He realized that he had caught up with not one, but both of the vehicles that were wanted in connection with a possible murder investigation. He wasn't a hundred percent sure if he was supposed to be proud or afraid.

As the man sat the shotgun down by his feet, Kyle took a step back to make sure he could cover all of the people at the scene. He had to radio in his location in case things turned bad. The bulletin hadn't given any details on the murder or how it had been committed. He had no idea which of these people were the suspect that he was looking for.

"We're just out here to have a nice, friendly conversation," said one of the men by the newer truck. He smiled. "Gun went off by accident."

56

Kyle gave the man a quick once over. He was thirty-ish and clean cut. He had the look of someone who worked out constantly. The muscles under his shirt rippled when he moved.

"This is Trooper Kyle," he said into his radio. "I've got both vehicles from that BOLO on the side of the US 60, five miles east of Wickliffe. Four suspects and a child on the scene. Requesting back up to my location."

"Roger that," dispatch replied.

"Horn here," another voice said. "I'm ten minutes out."

"Now we are all going to sit and wait," Kyle told them.

"There's no need in all of this fuss," said the man who had spoken earlier. He took a step away from the other and smiled. A shiver ran up the state trooper's spine. There was something predatory in that man's smile. "Why don't you get back in your cruiser and carry on?"

Kyle shifted his gaze between the spokesman and the others. The rest of the group seemed content to wait and see what happened. There was something different about this one. He was confident. Maybe too confident. He wasn't making some last ditch effort at escaping, he had it all planned out.

"Get back over there with your friends," Kyle ordered.

Instead the man took another step forward, holdings his palms out as if trying to show that he meant no harm. The trooper wasn't buying it. He was either trying to get close enough to make a grab for the gun, or he was trying to distract Kyle while one of the others made a move.

"Shut up and get back over there," Kyle snapped.

"This is your last warning. One more step and I will shoot you."

The man took another step forward, his grin widening.

"Go on and shoot then," the man said.

Kyle heard the man with the little girl tell her to look away, then he lost track of the rest. If the speaker had been trying to district him, it had worked, but he didn't think that was it. Every bit of his instinct told him to shoot, but the idea of shooting an unarmed man disgusted him. He hesitated.

"You don't have that killer instinct do you?" the approaching man asked.

He made a quick move as if to charge him, and this time Kyle did fire. The bullet struck the man in the center of the chest from only a half dozen feet away. It didn't take him down as he had expected. The man just continued to smile and looked down at his bleeding chest wound.

When he looked up his eyes were glowing a bright amber color.

Chapter Eight

Fire erupted from the muzzle of the trooper's sidearm, and Steve knew at once it was over. Kentucky State Troopers did not carry silver bullets as part of their arsenal, and that one ten millimeter was not enough to even slow the werewolf down. The trooper was already dead and didn't know it.

"Okay, you've wasted enough of my time," Owen growled.

The trooper, Kyle his name tag read, took a step back, putting the nose of his cruiser between himself and his soon to be attacker. He kept the gun leveled at Owen's chest. Steve could sense his fear, but the man hid it well.

"Daddy, I want to go home," Miranda whined.

"Close your eyes and cover your ears honey," Steve ordered. He took her by the shoulders and pushed her behind him.

With everyone else distracted, he reached down and picked up his shotgun. He knew he couldn't stop Owen from killing the trooper, but he might slow him down enough to let the man get away. He aimed the shotgun at the small of the alpha wolf's back and fired. The blast ripped through the back of Owen's shirt and peppered the front fender of the state police cruiser.

"I am getting really tired of you shooting me," Owen said. He turned to glare at Steve with his glowing eyes and bared fangs. "That is the last time, do you hear me? When I finish this, I am going to rip you and your precious little girl limb from limb."

Steve pumped the shotgun and fired again. This blast struck Owen in chest and throat. Blood gushed from the corners of his mouth, but a grin spread across his face. He took a step forward, momentarily forgetting the state trooper behind him. Steve was hoping the man

59

would take the chance to escape, but he didn't. He was either too stubborn or two dedicated to leave the scene of a shooting.

Although he was not running away, Trooper Kyle was apparently not taking any chances with his would-be attacker. He fired, striking Owen in the back of the head. His face was momentarily disfigured, and a stream of blood ran from the side of his already bloodshot eye.

He spun, changing as he moved. Steve had never seen the full change first hand, and it turned his stomach. Muscular shoulders ripped through Owen's shirt even as course hair began to spring through his skin. His jaw seemed to break loose and then started to extend into an elongated snout. His hand's seemed to become deformed, recreating themselves as giant claws.

Owen was fully changed into his werewolf form by the time he slammed into the side of the state police cruiser, crushing the front fender. He hit with such force that he knocked the wheels closest to him off the ground and sent Trooper Kyle sprawling on the ground. The state trooper opened fire, emptying a clip into the creature's chest.

Steve glanced back at the other werewolves, who were beginning to show signs of the change as well. Seeing Chloe with glowing eyes and sharp fangs was possibly the worst thing he'd seen. She had become something alien and dangerous. Something that wanted to hurt his little girl.

He lifted Miranda into his arms and started to run.

Sebastian Kyle cursed under his breath as the creature crept onto the hood of his car. In one smooth action he popped out the empty clip and slammed another one home. He rolled to his left, barely clearing the undercarriage of the cruiser enough to slide underneath it. Four giant claws slammed into the asphalt where he had been lying only a second before.

The creature turned, trying to shove it's snout under the cruiser. It stopped less than an inch from the trooper's face, close enough that he could feel it's hot breath on his skin. Razor sharp fangs gnashed at him. He aimed the muzzle of his service weapon into the thing's gapping mouth and started firing.

It jerked backwards, howling angrily at the sky, and at that moment his mind registered the reality that, as hard as it was to believe, he was facing a werewolf. His mind tried to run down what he knew about such creatures, which was very little. He had never spent much time watching horror movies or anything he considered make believe. Never once would he have thought that one day he would need to know how to survive a werewolf attack.

What he did know for sure was that a KSP issued service pistol was not going to kill a werewolf. For the first time in his career he began to think of ways to survive, and he could come up with very little. Nothing, really. There was no way he was going to either get into his car and drive away or get away on foot. He did not know if the other people out there were werewolves or not, but the only one who seemed inclined to help was the one with the kid.

Backup was still several minutes away, but they wouldn't be much help. They'd just end up dead too.

As the werewolf paced and howled beside his cruiser, he glanced towards the shoulder of the road where the two trucks were parked. He could see the feet of the creatures two companions on the opposite side of the newer truck, and beyond them, a drop off. He knew this section of road pretty well, having driven it most

61

of his life. That drop off would fall a dozen or so feet to a corn field. The best he could hope would be to lose the creature in the corn, but even that didn't seem very likely.

The werewolf stopped pacing and finally turned it's attention back to Kyle. Instead of trying to go under the car, it slammed into the side of it, lifting the driver's side into the air. It repeated the action a second time, lifting the car just a little higher.

He didn't wait for the third attempt, knowing full well that sooner or later the cruiser would turn over, and he would be caught. He rolled again, moving from the cruiser to the pickup. Behind him the creature struck the car and it flipped over, crashing onto it's side, right where his legs had been only a moment before. The light bar on top of the car broke loose and slammed into his leg. It hurt, but he didn't think there was any real damage.

Kyle rolled again, coming out at the feet of a large bearded man in camo and a pretty young woman in faded denim shorts. They both looked down at him with fiery eyes, but neither made a move. He cursed, rose to his knees and then lunged for the drop off. He struck the embankment and started barrel-rolling downhill.

Steve wasn't aware of the change overcoming him, but clearly some part of it had. With his daughter clutched in his arms, he was sprinting at a physically impossible rate of speed, leaving the altercation behind them. But even as he ran his heightened senses could track the trooper as he rolled first under his own cruiser, then under Owen's truck and finally made a desperate dive for freedom. He wished the man well, but he had more important business. He had to get his daughter to safety.

Ahead of him an antique black Rolls-Royce

turned off of the asphalt, into a gravel turn around, blocking his path. The driver, dressed in a black suit and driver's cap climbed out of the car and walked around to the back side facing Steve. He opened the door, then went back to the driver's seat.

"If you want to survive, I suggest you get in the car," a gravely female voice stated.

Steve didn't argue.

Kyle's bullet-proof vest probably saved him from killing himself on the way down the hill. During the fall he had struck several large rocks that jutted out of the dirt. As he lay in the mud, he was pretty sure he had broken several ribs, but the vest had prevented anything worse. He knew he needed to get moving, but it hurt to breath.

Back on top of the hill the creature howled again, and suddenly his cruiser came flying through the air. It flipped over the top of the jacked up pickup, rolled through mid-air and headed straight for him. Kyle struggled to his feet and stumbled out of the car's way. It landed on it's roof in the mud, taking out a few corn stalks.

His eyes spotted something in the darkness that gave him hope. Only a half dozen feet away was the mouth of a culvert that extended across highway 62 to the cornfield on the other side. Fighting for each breath he pressed on, stumbling through the mud. When he had reached the opening he dropped to his knees and started crawling.

The concrete culvert was barely big enough for him. His uniform scrapped the top and bottom as he inched forward, and for a moment he was afraid he'd get stuck in the opening. But he made it.

Behind him the werewolf landed with a splash next to the destroyed cruiser. It lunged for him but was a split second too late. The creature's claws sliced through the bottoms of his boots, but never broke skin.

Kyle used his knees and elbows to propel himself forward into the darkness. Under normal circumstance he would have worried about snakes or poisonous spiders that like to call cold, damp spaces home. Under these circumstances he was just glad to be alive. He would worry about snakes and spiders later.

Finally the pain in his ribs grew so bad that his body couldn't take it any more. He passed out as the werewolf howled from the opening of the culvert.

Chapter Nine

Steve sat in the back of the ancient Rolls-Royce with Miranda hugged against his chest. A grey haired woman who appeared as old as the vehicle sat across from him, her age spotted hands folded formally in her lap. She regarded them coolly with cold, grey eyes. An elaborate jeweled necklace hung around her neck, and although he knew little of jewelry, he would have guessed it was worth a fortune.

"I guess you are wondering who I am," she said,

"That's a good place to start," he said, sniffing the air. She didn't have to tell him what she was. Every inch of the car smelled of werewolves. Many werewolves. Possibly generations of them.

"My name is Elizabeth Shelley," the woman told him. "I've come to welcome you to my territory."

"You're the alpha?"

"I despise such terms," she told him. "Such words are human words, made popular in horribly written novels and bad movies. I prefer to be called Mrs. Shelley or simply ma'am. But, as to your question, I suppose you would say that I am the 'alpha' in the territory that you're entering. I control everything from here to the river and for another two dozen miles north and south."

"You seem a little more civilized than the others of our kind that I've met," he told her.

"You're still young," Elizabeth said. "Probably not even to your first full moon?" He nodded. "If you survive that, you'll meet others. The level of civility varies from group to group. The older families, such as mine, have retained our manners through the years. Some of the newer packs, well, they seem to have bought into the human image of the werewolf."

"Are you going to hurt us?"

The woman laughed, a sound that made Steve

65

smile despite himself. There was nothing dangerous or animalistic about this woman. If he couldn't smell her true scent, he would have just taken her for a kindly grandmother.

"We don't hurt anyone who doesn't deserve it," she said. "And as long as you are respectful while a guest in our territory, we wont allow anyone else to harm you either."

"Really?" he asked, shocked. "You mean you will protect me from the pack that is chasing me?"

"For a brief time," she said. "You are a guest here, not family, so you will have to move along in a day or two. But for that day or two you will be protected."

"Thank you so much," Steve told her. "If there is ever any way I can repay you, just let me know."

Elizabeth smiled. For a moment he thought he could come to love this woman. He smiled too, and for the first time since he'd told her to close her eyes, Miranda raised her head and looked at their host. Even she smiled.

"The pack that was following you...was your 'alpha' among them?" Elizabeth asked, making a face at her own use of the word.

"Yes," he replied. "Owen."

"So you turned your back on your creator?" she asked.

"He tried to...hurt...my daughter."

"Very interesting," the woman mused. "It is very uncommon for a young werewolf to stand against his master. Almost unheard of for one who hasn't even made it to his first full moon. That means you are...the two of you...very special. But you should know, this Owen will pursue you to the ends of the earth. The small packs like his that haven't earned their own territory yet are only allowed two members, and he already had two that were

66

standing with him. I assume you were a mistake?"

"He took me on a trip I wasn't supposed to come back from."

"This gets more interesting," she told him.

"He messed up and took me to a place I knew better than he did," Steve said. He glanced out the window as the Kentucky countryside slowly gave way to a few farm houses and finally some semblance of a neighborhood. "So if you're going to run me out of here in a day or two, I'm going to need my truck. If the police get there before I do, it'll be taken in as evidence."

Elizabeth leaned forward and knocked on the glass partition between the back seat and the driver. The glass eased down and Steve's nose caught the scent of another werewolf. He held back his surprise, pretty sure that he would be seeing a lot more of his kind over the next day or two.

"Samuel, please tell Marty to go pick up this man's pickup truck," she ordered. "Tell him to hurry, the state police will likely be on the scene in a matter of moments."

"Yes ma'am," the driver said.

"Get in the truck!" Owen ordered. He had changed back into his human form as he climbed the hill back to the road. He was naked and his body was covered with mud. His chest wound had already begun to heal.

He glared at Dave, suddenly questioning his selection of pack members. First Charles got himself killed, and now his number two just stood by while he fought with the cop. He had picked the two because of their size and rather vicious dispositions, but both men were somewhat lacking in the intelligence area. He almost laughed. That was an understatement. Dave and Charles were total idiots.

As he started the truck and turned back towards Paducah, he glanced at the girl in the rearview. She was something else. She might want him dead, but her will to kill him was easily bent by his authority as alpha. And the way she had off'd the werewolf they'd encountered in Pine Grove? Few new werewolves would have known to go for the heart. With her intelligence and instincts, once he managed to break her spirit, she would become a wonderful werewolf. Maybe even a good mate.

"You doing okay back there, honey?" he asked.

"Screw you," Chloe snapped.

Owen smiled. When they had finished this business with her husband, he really planned to get to work on her. Then he would kill Dave and they could start over. She could help him select the new members of the pack.

A tow truck blew past them, traveling well over the speed limit. He caught the faint scent of a werewolf, but paid little attention to it. They were very close to the territory of a very old pack, so there were probably werewolves all over the place.

A few minutes later he saw blue lights approaching and turned off onto a narrow country road.

The limo rolled into the small town of Wickliffe, Kentucky. Steve had passed through it a time or two, but he'd never paid much attention. It was just a small village set on the banks of the Mississippi River, right below the point where the Mississippi and Ohio joined, creating the "Mighty Mississippi" as it was known. The buildings were mostly old, classic brick structures that were all the craze around the last turn of the century. Several old colonial-style houses still stood, a throwback to the town's southern roots.

"Welcome to our home," Elizabeth said. "My

family has called this spot home for generations, Steve. Long before the first white man settled on this side of the Appalachians, my people had a thriving community here."

"You're Native American?"

"You'd never guess it by looking at me, but yes," she told him. "Most of our people died off or fled long ago, but my family stayed. We eventually married into the settlers and were all but assimilated into the European lifestyle."

"Were your people-?"

"Yes, my Native American ancestors were lycanthropes," Elizabeth said. "The term werewolf didn't come around until after the Europeans did. There used to be a lot of lycanthropes among the native people. At one time it was an honor, but things eventually got twisted. Even among the native peoples there were those like your friend back there. They had a total disregard for law and order. When they began slaughtering people, instead of being honored, we became demonized. All of us. They ran our kind out of villages all over the continent. The village that existed here was one of the last in North America."

"How is it that you've been able to survive here?"

"Most of the native people left here by 1300 or so," she explained. "My people, the lycanthropes, stayed. As the other tribes began to turn on their own, we welcomed them. Or at least the ones who agreed to follow the rules. When the white people came we married into their families and carried on. Most of the white people didn't believe, so we had nothing to worry about as long as every followed the rules."

"You keep talking about rules," Steve said. "Who makes and enforces these rules?"

69

"The elders council," Elizabeth said. "There were six elders to begin with, all rooted in one of the native tribes. A few white lycanthropes wandered in eventually, and we welcomed them to the council as well. Then some of the tribes that had not cast their werewolves out reached out to us. They'd heard what we were doing and wanted to be a part. When it was all said and done we had twelve elders on the council, each the leader of a pack."

"That is a lot of werewolves in one place."

"And that was the problem," she admitted. "It was decided that each of the packs would relocate. The Native Americans mostly went back to their reservations and rejoined their tribes, or they went to their native lands to live as white people. The European packs went to find new lands."

"So where does Owen fit in?"

"Its not often I have a need to explain all of this," Elizabeth interrupted. "We don't see many of the new packs here. Those we do see are just passing through. We mind our business and they mind theirs."

"New packs?"

"Eventually, even after spreading out, the old packs outgrew their lands," she said. "You see, werewolves like you are in the minority. Most werewolves are born, not created. Occasional a member of a pack will fall in love with an outsider and they'll be granted membership, but other than that, you never see half breeds in the old packs."

Steve felt the spite in her voice when she used the term 'half breeds'. For the first time in his life he was learning what it felt like to be in a minority, and he wasn't very fond of that feeling. But, he knew, there was nothing that he could do about it. Like it or not, Owen had turned him into a monster and he was going to have

70

to fit into their culture one way or another.

"Three or four years ago the elders allowed a few of their more...unsatified members to start their own packs," she recalled. "They were limited to three underlings. Ideally each one would create a pack made up of two male and two female, that way the pack would grow naturally. It would also create reason for them to settle somewhere and blend in. But what actually happened is that most of the new packs decided to fill their ranks with strong males. Instead of settling, they roam the country killing indiscriminately because without mates, the males are always fighting amongst themselves.

"The council decided to put a stop to it and issued the order that no new male werewolves were to be made without their permission."

"So that's why he wants me dead?"

"Yes, he did not need permission to change the girl, but you...you are evidence of his crime," Elizabeth told him.

"I'm done playing with this guy," Owen said as he piloted his truck back towards Paducah. "Seriously, he's been a werewolf for less than twenty-four hours and he's already enlisted the help of another pack?"

"Which pack is in this area?" Dave asked.

"The Shelley's," Owen said. "Old pack. Old money. Old sense of morality. The old broad that runs the pack thinks this is the old south and she's freakin' Scarlet O'Hara or something."

"So what do we do?"

"We wait. We find some place to crash for the night, and tomorrow I'll make some calls. Maybe I can get my old alpha to get me a meeting with the old lady."

They drove in silence for several minutes. When they were nearly into town they had to pull over as a group of emergency vehicles raced in the direction of Wickliffe.

Chapter Ten

The limo turned into the driveway of a massive plantation-style house that stood on a hillside overlooking the Mississippi River. The lawn was as meticulously maintained as any Steve had ever seen. Concrete wolf statues dotted the lawn, mostly surrounded by flowers and rose bushes. It seemed that every light in the house was on, and he could make out a number of shadows in the windows.

"Welcome to my estate," Elizabeth said. "My grandfather was something of a shipping magnate in the late eighteen hundreds. We've scaled back, but we still do a good business moving cargo around the country."

Miranda stirred in his arms, opening her eyes in time to see the big house looming before them. She looked at it with wide eyes and grinned.

"Castle?" she asked.

"No darlin, but it is a very nice house," he told her, hugging her to his chest. "It belongs to our new friend, Mrs. Shelley."

Miranda looked from the house to Mrs. Shelley and continued to grin. It was infectious, and by the time the car rolled to a stop, all three of them were smiling. For Steve, it was a relief to push everything else out of his mind for just a moment and focus on his daughter. In the last twenty-four hours she had seen things that would challenge even the toughest person's sanity, including seeing her mother turn into a werewolf, and yet she seemed unphased by it.

"I think its a castle," she said as they pulled to a stop by the front door.

"It can be what ever you want it to be, darling," Elizabeth said. She reached over and patted the little girl on the hand. Miranda in turn looked up to her father for guidance.

"It's okay, she is our friend," Steve said.

The driver, Samuel, came around and opened the rear passenger door to the car. Steve sat Miranda down on the concrete and stepped out after her. A moment later Elizabeth climbed out with a grace and ease that was unusual in someone her age. She saw Steve looking and smiled.

"There are some nice aspects of being a lycan," she told him with a smile. Then she knelt down next to Miranda. "I have several great grandchildren your age that would love to make a new friend. Do you think you would like that?"

"Yeah!" Miranda said. Then, for just a second, her smile faded and she looked quizzically up at her father. "Please daddy?"

"Mr. Slate," Elizabeth said, gently taking him by the arm before he could answer. "I can sense your hesitation before you even say anything. I assure you, you are both one hundred percent safe while you are in our home. None of my pack will hurt you, and we will fight tooth and nail to protect you from anyone who would."

Steve looked down at Miranda. He wanted to see her smile again, so he nodded.

"Thank you!" she cheered, wrapping her arms around his legs.

The inside of the house was as classically decorated as the plantation-style exterior deserved. Everything looked very old and very expensive. Miranda clutched his hand as they walked through the house to where a grand staircase led up to the second floor. A butler in a dark coat stood at the foot of the stairs, a smile on his face.

"Marvin, Mr. Slate and his daughter, Miranda, will be our guests for a day or two," Elizabeth said.

"Very pleased to have you," the man said. Steve sniffed the air and was surprised to find that the man was not a werewolf. "I will prepare the guest suite."

"Wonderful," the lady of the house said. "Are the kids in the playroom?"

"Yes they are, ma'am."

"Would you be so kind as to escort Miss Miranda to the play room then?"

Steve watched his daughter as she climbed the stairs, now holding hands with Mrs. Shelley's butler.

Elizabeth personally ushered Steve into her study. The room was larger than any room in his own house, and the walls were lined with thick, leather bound books. On some of the spines he saw the names of celebrated classical authors, among them the wordsmith of the Mississippi himself, Mark Twain. There were also an assortment of law and deed books. The few spots on the wall that weren't covered with books had been covered with photographs, many of them old. A few looked to be from the Civil War era, printed on metal rather than paper.

He saw nothing that told of the family's history as werewolves, but several glass display cases showed items that were definitely connected. They appeared to be relics of various werewolf hunters throughout history. A silver tipped spear hung on one wall. One display case contained a hand-carved bow and an assortment of silver tipped arrows. Inside another case were two ancient Colt .45s and a few dozen silver tipped bullets.

The lady of the house sat behind a large oak desk that looked as if it never had and never would hold a computer. The window behind her had a magnificent view of the Mississippi as it flowed by extreme Western Kentucky. Seated in her spot with her hands folded casually on the desktop, it was easy for him to see that she was a person of breeding and status.

"We will do what we can to help you," Elizabeth assured him. "You must understand, this is a very peculiar situation that we find ourselves in. The full moon is this Saturday. You can't be here when it happens. My pack would never accept a new outsider during that sensitive time. If you weren't new, then there would be no problem. But since you are..."

Steve stared at her as she trailed off. Owen and Dave had said that he would never survive the full moon on his own, and now the only werewolf he knew who didn't want him dead was telling him he had to go. But his first thought wasn't of himself, it was of his daughter. He wanted to survive for her. He wanted her to grow up with a father.

"So what happens on Saturday?"

"You know the legends about werewolves and the full moon," she said. "There is some accuracy in them. The animal part of us is always present, hidden somewhere below our civilized human exteriors. That part is never closer to the surface than it is on the full moon. On that night it wants out. It needs out."

"So why is this so dangerous for me? I haven't fully changed yet, but I've changed a little."

"Your first full moon is the most dangerous. You and the wolf are two different beings struggling for dominance. Right now Steve Slate is the dominant being because it is your body. On Saturday, when the moon frees the wolf from it's bonds, it will try to take control. If it does, you will be destroyed. There will be nothing left of the man who was, just a blood thirsty, snarling monster."

"How do I stop it?" he asked.

"I don't know," Elizabeth admitted. "Normally, the pack will band together and the leader will use his dominance to keep the wolf in check. In your case, you have no 'alpha' as you would say. There will be nothing to prevent the wolf from taking over."

They stared at each other silently as the words sank in. Steve had trouble believing it, but two days earlier he would not have believed that werewolves really existed. He faught back the urge to panic. He still had to save Miranda, whether or not he made it through the coming full moon didn't matter if he did not get her to safety.

"So what happens when it does?" Steve asked,

"First, you'll kill your daughter," she said. "And then, until your body gives out or until you are killed, you will kill anyone and anything you encounter."

"Wolves are not solitary animals," she continued. "In the wild wolves live in packs, hunt in packs and protect their own in packs. A wolf on it's own rarely survives. Sometimes the younger wolves will force older, weaker alphas out of the pack in order to take charge. But on occasion you will find a wolf that leaves of it's own free will. Maybe it doesn't like the hierarchy of the pack, or maybe it's antisocial. Those wolves are called disperser. They live on the fringes of established packs or in the areas where several packs' territories come together."

"Do they survive?"

"Sometimes," Elizabeth said. "The meanest and strongest survive. The others...not so much. The packs do not generally like disperser. Their solitary nature goes against everything that the pack believes in and fights for. They're often hunted down and killed to keep them from trying to move in on a pack's territory."

"So is that what I can expect?" Steve asked. "I don't just have to worry about Owen Black, I have to worry about every other pack on the planet?"

"Dear, just worry about making it through the weekend," she told him. "If, somehow you make it through the full moon, then you can worry about what the packs are going to do to you."

Chapter Eleven

Tad Tuttle and Mark Rollins rolled to a stop behind a police barricade on highway 62, just outside the city of Wickliffe. Four state police cruisers were blocking the west bound lane, while a sheriff's deputy was waving traffic through, one car at a time. Off to their right the shoulder dropped off a dozen feet or so to a corn field, where a number of troopers were gathered around the wreckage of one of their cruisers.

"This doesn't look promising," Rollins said.

"You can say that again," Tad replied as he climbed out of the Pine Grove police cruiser.

The bank's security camera angle was wrong to see anything beyond the entrance to Red's parking lot, but it had been good enough for he and Rollins to identify both Steve Slate and Owen Black as they turned into Red's parking lot. Slate left the parking lot a half hour before Black arrived on the scene, but Wayne Shelley's big rig had pulled in only seconds after Black. That put Black at the scene of the truck driver's death. They didn't have enough to consider it a murder yet, but with the man's heart being ripped out, he didn't see any way it could prove to be anything else.

Tad slowly made his way down the slope towards the cornfield. The bank was uneven and hidden beneath the grass and dirt was a thick layer of big rocks that made the going harder. The rock's threatened to shift with each step, worsening the odds that he was going to tumble down the hill and break his neck.

Despite all odds, he finally arrived at the bottom, where he was greeted by a state trooper. He quickly checked their IDs and pointed them towards the officer in charge, a big barrel chested trooper named Miles Smith. Miles was directing the crime scene unit that was carefully searching the wrecked cruiser.

79

"Evening gentlemen," Miles said. "Welcome to Ballard County."

"No sign of your trooper?" Tad asked.

"Not yet, but I'm sure Kyle will turn up," the trooper said. "Looks like there were a lot of shots fired up top, but not much blood. Kyle is an excellent marksman, so I really doubt he missed. That means we might be dealing with someone wearing body armor. You see any evidence of that at your scenes?"

"We're still not sure what we've got in Miltonboro," Tad told him. "I got one house that looks like the US Army used it for target practice, and another that looks like there was a bar fight in it. We've got enough blood for a dead body, but no body."

"And I've got some guy with his heart ripped out," Rollins added. "ID said he was from Wickliffe."

"No crap?" Miles said, taking a step away from the cruiser. "Who was it?"

"Guy named Wayne Shelley."

"Wayne?" Miles asked, clear recognition sounding in his voice. "He's family. You mean to tell me the guys who shot it out with Trooper Kyle took out Wayne Shelley?"

"Looks that way," Rollins said.

Miles pressed the palm of his hand to his chin, suddenly lost in thought. Tad and Rollins exchanged a look, both suddenly sure that the trooper knew something he was not going to tell them.

"I need to go tell his mom," Miles said at last. "You're sure it was Wayne?"

"We've got an ID from his driver's license," Rollins said. "Still need someone to officially identify the body, but I saw it for myself. It's him."

"Probably need to excuse myself from this investigation anyway," the trooper said absently.

80

"You mind if I ride along?" Rollins asked.

"I'd prefer if you didn't," Miles said. "This is kinda personal."

"I understand, sir, but as Mr. Shelley's death is my case, I really need to speak with his next of kin," Rollins argued. "That might go over a little easier if I get an introduction from a member of the family."

Tad watched as Detective Rollins and Miles drove away in the big trooper's cruiser. The man knew something, he was sure of that, but he didn't seem like he was going to be coughing that information up any time soon. Maybe after talking with the family he might change his tune.

He turned away from the crime scene guys and clicked on his Maglight. Tad shone it up the hill towards the road. There were a lot of disturbances on the hillside, but most of that could have been from law enforcement personnel that had been going up and down. He hoped the crime scene unit had photographed the hill before they had started descending.

Near the base of the hill be saw a disturbance in the mud. Shining his light carefully in his path to make sure he didn't step on any evidence, he started working his way in that direction. Other than the tracks that looked like they belonged to the crime scene people, he didn't see anything heading in the direction of the wreckage. If trooper Kyle had been in the car when it came down the hill, either he would have had to walk out under his own power or be carried out by someone else. There was no sign of either.

He recognized the paw prints before he reached his destination. They were the same large prints he had seen at the original crime scene and at the Black house. He couldn't imagine the size of the animal that had made those tracks. It was something that definitely would be noticed if someone were keeping it as a pet.

The tracks led further away from the car, towards a drainage culvert that ran under the highway. He followed them, being careful to not step on any of the tracks. He had a growing suspicion that they would become very important to the investigation. If nothing else they tied all three cases together.

The animal had scratched and clawed at the ground near the opening as if it had been trying to get inside, turning up a lot of mud and dirt.

He knelt down and shined his light into the culvert. A half dozen feet inside he saw the destroyed soles of a man's boots.

"I think I found your trooper!" he yelled, and the crime scene guys came running.

Chapter Twelve

Elizabeth's grandchildren had a playroom that was nearly this size of Steve's backyard, and in the center was an elaborate playhouse that was a perfect replica of their grandmother's plantation house. Miranda and three other children all fit inside, where they were laughing and giggling amongst themselves. Despite everything else that had happened in the last twenty-four hours, the sound of his daughter laughing was enough to make him smile.

Steve had always wanted to be a father. But a half dozen years into their marriage, doctors had told them that Chloe would never be able to have a baby. There had been a lot of tears and even some harsh words from both of them, yet in the end they had stuck it out and decided to move on. They had explored adoption as one avenue, but neither of them felt right about it. While they admired anybody who could adopt, they calmly accepted the fact that it was not for them, meaning they would spend the rest of their lives childless.

Then one day Chloe had been waiting for him when he got home from work, a pregnancy test in her hand. The symbol was a plus sign, and from then on their lives had been changed.

His own father had been a good man, but he and Steve had never been close. He hadn't enjoyed all of the things that had been a part of who his father. Rick their father's son, had been all about hunting and fishing. He'd spent most of his high school career skipping school so he could get more time in the woods, and their father had not only been okay with it. He'd drive him to the woods. On the other hand, their father had never once came to one of Steve's baseball games.

The day he had learned he was going to be a father, Steve had vowed that he would always be there for

83

his little one, it didn't matter what their interests ended up being. So far he always had been, but now he didn't know how things were going to turn out. There was no way he could have prepared for this. Who would have imagined that one day he would be a werewolf?

Miranda popped her head out of one of the play-house's chimney's and waved at him. He waved back and she smiled. Then she disappeared back inside with a giggle.

A young woman in an ankle length skirt stepped through the doorway into the playroom, looking as if she had just come from some church function. She smiled politely at Steve and walked straight to the playhouse. He thought she looked four or five years younger than him, and she was very pretty. She had a dark complication, which gave her a slightly Italian look.

"Harold! Ginger! Mollie!" she called into the playhouse. Three little heads popped up from inside the playhouse. "Marvin just told me that we had a guest. I want you to treat her very nicely, you understand?"

"Yes, mommy!" they said in unison.

She smiled, seeming satisfied with that answer, and turned towards Steve.

"I promise you she will be safe with my little ones," she told him, then stuck out her hand, which he shook. "Allison Booth, Mr. Slate. Elizabeth is my grand-mother."

"Nice to meet you."

"Of course, but I wish it were under other cir-cumstances," the girl continued. "I want you to know, we do not believe in turning people against their will. What these people have done to you and your family is unforgivable."

"I agree."

"I would think so," she said with a laugh. "My

84

husband, Marty, is a mechanic. He picked up your truck before the authorities arrived and said he can have it ready to leave by tomorrow morning. That will give you two days to get to where you need to go to get your daughter safe."

"I really appreciate it," he told her.

"I wish there was more we could do," Allison said. She folded her hands neatly in front of her. "But we will keep you safe until your truck is ready. Maybe we can slow down those who are chasing you as well."

"That would be very helpful."

"Not all of our kind are like that, Mr. Slate," Allison told him. "But, sadly, many of them are. It's been that way for as long as our people have recorded their history. I would love to see it change...but I don't see that happening any time soon. The old alphas, like Grannie, are still strong and set in their ways. And the young alphas are like the ones chasing you. Cocky. Mean. They think they own the world and everyone in it."

"When I was in Miss Elizabeth's office, I saw a gun in there with silver bullets," Steve said. "Any chance she would let me borrow that for a few days?"

"I really doubt that, sir," she told him. "That gun is a very important relic for our family. Grannie's grandfather took that off of the last werewolf hunter that was ever seen in the United States. He was a very deadly man, and killed two dozen members of our pack. Nearly wiped us out."

Steve nodded thoughtfully. He'd known it would be a long shot, but he needed to ask. Where else would he find silver bullets? He didn't care what they told him about there full moon, he had every intention of coming back and killing Owen Black one way or the other. Black was a monster and he deserved to die.

"Sometimes the difference in who is bad and who

is good is which side of the fight you're on," Steve said.

"Very true," Allison said with a smile. She sat quietly for a long time, and then her smile faded. "Mr. Slate, whatever you hear while you are here...whatever she tells you...don't believe it. Our family has a dark side that they try to keep hidden, but the truth is that my grandmother is not a very nice person. If you get the chance, get your family out of here as quickly as you can."

"Daddy, can we stay here?" Miranda asked as he carried her into their bedroom. She wrapped her arms around his neck and squeezed. "Pwease?"

"I'm sorry, baby, we are going to have to leave for Uncle Rick's after breakfast," he told her. "Daddy's got to do something, and he won't be able to take you with him."

"You'll find mommy?" she asked.

"I'm going to try," he told her.

"And you will bring her home?"

"That's the plan," he said. He laid her down on the big four poster bed, and for just a moment she forgot what they had been talking about. "It's a princess bed!"

She climbed up on her little legs and started jumping up and down. He knew he needed to reprimand her, but at the moment he didn't care. Both of her parents had been turned into werewolves and she'd nearly been killed twice, all in the same day. If she wanted to jump on the bed he was going to let her.

"Daddy, will mommy try to eat me?" she asked, her face suddenly getting very serious in only the way a small child's can.

"No, baby," he lied. "When I bring her home, she wont want to hurt you."

Well, it was a partial lie. If he did manage to both

86

survive and bring Chloe home, he was going to be absolutely positive that she wasn't going to be a threat to their daughter. He really didn't think that would be a problem, though, because until Owen had ordered her to attack, she had been fine. But he was still new to this. He really had no idea how any of this worked.

Steve crawled into bed, and Miranda snuggled up against him.

"Can we play the monster game, daddy?"

"Honey, I think it's too late to be playing games," Steve said. "And haven't you had enough monsters today?"

"Not real monsters, daddy!" she said with a laugh.

He smiled. "Just your hand!"

"Okay, okay," he told her. He held up his hand and made it bark like a dog.

"That's a dog, not a monster!" Miranda protested.

"Okay, fine," Steve said, smiling. He made a growling noise as his hand snapped at her nose.

"Bad monster," she said to his hand. Then she held up her own little hands and made a whining sound. "Daddy! Daddy! We're your baby monsters."

"Hello baby monsters!"

They played for a few more minutes before she fell asleep in his arms.

A half hour later there was a knock at the door. He got up quietly, careful not to wake his daughter from her dreams. He cracked the door and peered out. Elizabeth stood in the hallway, smiling.

"I thought you might like to join me for a drink," she offered.

Steve glanced back at Miranda sleeping sideways in the bed. He hadn't realized how much he had missed her sleeping in the same bed with he and Chloe. Everyone said you needed to break your kids from sleeping with you as soon as possible, but for a moment he wondered if those people had ever had children.

"She will be fine, I promise," Elizabeth said. "We need to discuss your plans. Although I am sorry for what you've gone through, and I despise the one who would force this on someone, I have no ill will against you."

"I appreciate that," he said as he pulled the door quietly shut.

"First things first, you have to do something about your daughter," she said as they headed down the hall towards her study. "Although the odds are stacked against you, there is a slim chance that you could survive the full moon. You've already shown yourself to be both resourceful and powerful by disobeying an order from your creator and by evading him as long as you did. But if you are alone with her when the full moon comes and the wolf takes over, all will be lost. The wolf only respects the hierarchy of the pack. To it Miranda be will nothing but meat."

"I'm trying to get her to my brother's house in Arkansas," Steve told her. "If I can get back on the road, we can be there before the full moon."

"Good," she said as she pushed open the door to her study. Two coffee cups were already set out and poured. "That brings me to my second thought. What do you plan to do about your wife?"

Steve stared at her for a moment as they took their seats. He didn't have a clue. Once Miranda was safe he had every intention of getting Chloe back, but he didn't know how. It would, no doubt, involve killing both Owen and Dave. He had stood up to them once, but that time he'd had the element of surprise. On the other hand, he'd also had to worry about saving his daughter's life. It she was safely out of the picture he didn't have to worry about that.

"Of course you'll go after her," Elizabeth said at last. "Family is very important to you, that is very clear, but I don't think you can stand against them as a wolf. Your best bet would be to face them as a man."

"And how do I do that?"

"I think you already know. Allison told me you were asking about my collection. Silver really is used to kill werewolves. Or at least it was when there were still werewolf hunters roaming the earth. It's not magic, as it appears in movies. It's a simple allergic reaction."

She opened the case that contained the wooden bow and carefully plucked one of the silver tipped arrows from it's spot. Elizabeth stared at the shiny tip as she lovingly caressed the arrow's wooden shaft.

"Lycans are not immortal," she said. "We simply have a very high metabolism and the ability to heal ourselves very quickly. Theoretically you could kill one of us by dismemberment, or if you dropped us from a high enough airplane. The damage would have to be so severe that our body's healing qualities couldn't heal faster than death could arrive. You could blow us up, if we were close enough to the explosion. But in most cases none of these things are possible because we are stronger and faster than anyone who would be trying to kill us. Silver, though, is the great equalizer."

She held the tip of the arrow out in front of him and smiled.

"My ancestors collected these relics from the last of their kind," she said. "The last of the great werewolf hunters."

"Who were they?"

"A group of humans born with almost supernatural skills," Elizabeth said as she examined the arrow

89

carefully. "They had an unnatural knack for showing up anywhere there were beings that were not quite human. They were determined, aggressive and almost obsessive with ridding the earth of anything they considered 'unnatural'."

"Anything...?"

"Well you don't believe that we are alone, do you?" she asked.

"Two days ago I didn't believe werewolves were real," Steve told her.

"That's the great blessing of our existence," Elizabeth said. "When science replaced mythology, it became a lot easier to explain things away with science than to admit that there were so-called supernatural explanations. Werewolves. Vampires. Zombies. Demons. We were all the targets of the hunter's wrath."

"What happened to them?" he asked.

"Don't really know," she said with a shrug. "By the end of the 1800s there were only a few left world wide. Maybe they got killed off, or more likely, the younger generations bought into the myth that we weren't real. Either way, the last known hunter came here, and now his weapon is on display."

"So silver is the key?" he asked, pointing at the arrow. "Why silver?"

"If I stabbed you in the leg with this, it wouldn't kill you, but you would experience pain in the wound as if you were human," Elizabeth told him. "Even if you pulled it out, the wound would be very slow healing. It would take you nearly as long to heal as it would a human with a similar wound. You'd be wounded. Slow moving. An easy target for me to move in for the kill."

"What about the heart?"

"That really depends," she said. "It isn't an automatic kill, as the movies make it out to be. But it is the most likely way to kill a lycan. If the damage to the organ is severe enough, then your heart would not be able to heal before you bled to death. And to make matters worse, as your heart is struggling to keep pumping blood throughout your body, it would be circulating the silver through your veins. While not fatal, that makes you weak, sluggish and slows down your resistance to other injuries. With a silver arrow in your heart, for instance, it might be possible to inflict some severe damage to the rest of your body with a shotgun."

"So I need to get a silver weapon? Where exactly do I find one of those?"

"There are plenty of places out there, but it will take some time. Humans are obsessed with vampires, werewolves and zombies, even though they think that we're a myths. There are a surprising number of people who like to collect functioning sliver bullets, swords, bolts...pretty much anything that was ever used against us. You could probably find a dozen dealers on the internet."

"That doesn't help me now," Steve said.

Chapter Thirteen

The door to Elizabeth's study opened and Marvin stepped in. His face was flushed and Steve could hear his heart pounding. At first she gave the butler a surprised and somewhat annoyed look, but upon seeing his face, her expression changed to one of concern. She rose quickly to her feet.

"Ma'am, your nephew, Miles, is asking to see you," Marvin said. "I...I apologize for the interruption, but he says it is an emergency. He told me to interrupt you no matter what you were doing."

"It's quite alright," she assured the man, patting him on the shoulder. "Mr. Slate, Marvin will show you to the playroom if you would like to check on your daughter. I have some family business to attend to."

"Thank you for the talk," Steve said, getting to his feet. "I hope we have the time to talk some more later."

"I'm sure," Elizabeth said, dismissively.

"This way please, Mr. Slate," the butler said, motioning towards the door.

Steve stepped out into the small sitting room, where a large state trooper was waiting impatiently. With his werewolf senses he could hear the man struggling to control his breathing as if he were trying to hold back the change. When their eyes met the man's eyes flashed red and he bared his fangs.

As soon as they passed, the trooper barged into the study. He didn't bother to close the door, so Steve managed to pick up part of the conversation.

"Aunt Liz, Wayne is dead," the trooper said.

"Wayne?" she gasp. He could almost feel the sadness in her voice. "No, not my baby. It can't be Wayne, you've got to be wrong."

"I'm sorry, Aunt Liz, I really am," the big man

said. "There's a cop downstairs from Pine Grove, and he...he said someone or something had ripped Wayne's heart right out of his chest. It had to be a lycan."

Even from a dozen feet down the hall Steve could feel the sudden change in her. The mild mannered southern lady was gone, replaced by the true leader of her pack. When she spoke again the werewolf was in her voice and the sadness had been replaced by anger.

"Who did it?" she snarled.

"Police were investigating a murder and possible kidnapping in some little town called Miltonboro. The suspects headed west, through Pine Grove, where they ran into Wayne."

"Who was it?"

"I...I'm not sure," the man stammered. "They are looking for two guys." Steve could hear him fumbling with a notebook. "Owen Black and Steve Slate."

"Marvin!" Elizabeth roared. "Bring him back."

This time Marvin closed and bolted the door to the study when he left. Elizabeth stood at the window, struggling to control herself. The big trooper wasn't struggling so hard. His muscles were already struggling against the fabric of his uniform, and he was impatiently moving from foot to foot as if ready to pounce.

"I know it wasn't you," Elizabeth said at last. She turned away from the window, once again under control. "You don't have his blood on you or I would have smelt it. That means it was your creator. This...Owen Black."

"You mean one of the suspects is here, in your house?" the cop snarled. He took a step towards Steve, but Elizabeth shoved him backwards so hard that he flew into a book case, knocking a handful of books off the shelf.

"Steve is not the enemy," she said. "But he does

94

know this Owen Black. Tell us everything you know from the moment you met him."

Steve told them the abbreviated version, starting with the day Owen moved into their neighborhood and ending with the standoff on the side of the highway. At some point during the story the trooper regained some control and started scribbling notes in his book. They had several questions about Owen and Dave, but he had few answers. He wasn't sure where the man had come from, and he wasn't sure where he would go.

"The only thing I really heard was bits and pieces of a discussion he had with Dave, the other member of his pack," Steve told them. "He said something about his old pack having an altercation with someone called 'the Moon Dog' that resulted in a member of the pack being shipped back in pieces."

"Agleska," Elizabeth said, her face blank. "The lizard. He is the leader of the Lakota pack. A few years ago a member of his pack was killed in Mississippi. The killer shipped the poor boy's body back in a few dozen boxes."

"The Moon Dog?" Miles asked doubtfully.

"Oh, he is real, but I'd better never hear you repeat that," she ordered. "He's mad. He lives alone in the swamp and will kill any lycan that comes within a hour of his home territory. We leave him alone and he leaves us alone."

"One wolf? Why don't we just kill him?"

"Because we would pay a very heavy price for that one death," she said. "It is easier just to stay out of southern Mississippi. But none of that matters. I will contact Agleska, you worry about finding Owen Black and his pack."

"I will find them," the man growled.

95

"Miles, you will take them alive," she warned the younger man. "This is not something for you nor I to decide on our own. This is a decision for the council. Owen Black might have his own pack, but his is still sponsored by the Lakota. Killing him in retribution could be taken as an attack on Agleska and his pack. We do not want war."

"Fine."

"The council will not convene until after the full moon, so bring them back and we will lock them in the cages. After the council meets, we will kill them all one way or another."

"My wife is with them," Steve said.

The other two glared at him, and he saw in their eyes that they didn't care. They would hold her just as liable as the other two members of the pack. He felt the wolf stir within him, but pushed it down. He couldn't worry about Chloe now, not until he knew that Miranda was safe. Once he got her to his brother's, then he would find a way to save his wife.

"We will keep your wife with the others until the council meets," Elizabeth told him. "After that, it will be out of our hands."

"What if they don't come easy?"

"Accidents do happen, Miles, but I would prefer if they did not in this case. Especially with this Owen Black."

"I'm going with you to find them," Steve said.

"Mr. Slate, leave this to us."

He wasn't aware he was going to do it until he was done, and then it was too late to go back. For just a second Steve let go of his grip and felt the wolf surge forward. The room snapped into mind blowing clarity. It was as if, in a heartbeat, his world had made the jump from an old black and white television to LED high definition. He was aware of everything around him, from the other wolves' breathing to the blood flowing through their veins. He felt the swelling in his own muscles as they swelled and expanded.

"She is my wife, and I will take her alive," he snarled. Much to his surprise, the other wolves both took a step back in surprise. "I will not have your pack killing her accidently."

He thought that Elizabeth would lash out at him for disrespecting her, but instead he saw a glimmer of respect pass over her face. Respect and maybe even a little fear. They hadn't expected him to show such power, he could read that on their faces, although he really did not know exactly what it meant. He didn't know if it were something they would honor or seek to destroy.

"Very well," she replied after a long pause. "Miles, we will take care of this officer you have downstairs, and then we will deal with the matter at hand. Steve will go with you and the pack. Treat him as a guest, but if he gets out of line, you have my permission to destroy him." She looked at him and smiled. "Sorry, Mr. Slate, but if you want to run with the big dogs, you have to run under our rules."

Chapter Fourteen

Much to everyone's surprise, Sebastian Kyle was a bit shaken up, but otherwise he appeared unharmed. After being checked out by EMTs, he made a brief and vague report to the senior officer on the scene. He explained how he had spotted the two suspect vehicles on the side of the road. He told them that Steve Slate seemed to be trying to protect his daughter from Owen Black and two other unknowns, and that Slate had discharged a shotgun while trying to protect him from Black.

"It looked like he hit him, but he just kept coming," Kyle said. As he spoke, his eyes took on a thousand yard stare. "I fired my weapon several times, and I know I hit him. But he wouldn't go down. I'm not sure if he was wearing body armor or if he was loaded up on crank. Either way, nothing seemed to slow him down."

Tad Tuttle watched the interview from the background. He noted the absence of anything about large dogs or wolves, something that surely would have stood out in the man's mind, even if he was in shock. Trooper Kyle was holding something back. For some reason he did not want to mention the animals. He also claimed to not remember how his cruiser got at the bottom of the hill.

He was a little relieved to hear that Steve Slate appeared to be a victim. He might not know the man very well, but he didn't want to be forced to arrest an old team mate for murder.

Finally the other troopers patted Kyle on the back and someone handed him a cup of coffee. They all wandered back down to the wrecked car while Kyle took a seat on the hood on one of the cruisers. His eyes continued to stare into nothingness. Tad moved closer, watching the man closely.

"What about the dogs?" Tad asked once they

99

were alone.

When Kyle looked up, his face was filled with terror. His once blank eyes had gone wide. He nearly dropped his coffee cup as he jumped to his feet. For a moment he stammered and stuttered, unable to find any words. Finally he lied.

"There weren't any dogs."

"I know they were here, I saw their tracks," Tad said. "I also saw them in Pine Grove and in Miltonboro. Were they some kind of attack dogs?"

"Listen to me," Kyle warned. "You don't want to know. Just drop it and leave me alone. I'm alive. I'm going to go home and forget this ever happened."

"Help me out here, I've got a young man and his three year old on the run, and I don't even know what they're running from."

Kyle sipped his coffee as he dropped back onto the front of the cruiser. His eyes went back to staring blindly down the highway. Tad had no intention of letting up, and maybe the trooper sensed that. He sighed and his shoulders sagged.

"I'll tell you everything, but if you ever tell it to anyone else, I will deny it until my dying day," the man said.

"That's good enough for me," Tad told him. "We'll keep this between the two of us, but if you have something that might save that little girl, then tell me."

"Those weren't people," Kyle said. "Owen Black and the other two, they weren't people. They were monsters. Werewolves I think."

"Werewolves?"

Any rational human being would have automatically dismissed Sebastian Kyle as crazy. Tad Tuttle was no longer your average rational human being. That had

100

passed several years ago when he had been working another case. The biggest case of his life, really. It was the one that had eventually assured him of the promotion to detective, although in truth, he had done very little to deserve it.

Tad had been partnered with a state trooper named Greg Wyatt. Together the two of them had been hunting a serial killer known as "the peppermint man." The case had been bizarre from the start, and had stayed that way right up until Wyatt had cornered and killed a young man named Billy Jones in the local hospital. Experts said the boy had suffered a break from reality, but Wyatt had always insisted that Jones had been possessed.

Despite his own rational mind, Tad believed him, so werewolves were only a little bit of a stretch. As he listened to Kyle talk, he still was not convinced, but he was ruling nothing out. He would never put it in a police report, and he would probably never tell it to another soul, but he was willing to accept the possibility. If he managed to see one of them with his own eyes, he would officially believe it, until then it was just a theory.

"I shot him dead center of the chest and he wouldn't go down," Kyle told him. "I know I told the others that he might have been wearing a vest, but that was a lie. I shot him and I saw the blood from the wound. That was when he started to change. It made him mad. I still don't know how or why I got away. Maybe they saw my backup coming and ran away."

"What about Slate and the little girl?"

"I really have no idea, man. When I went off the side of the hill, I think they were still by that old truck. For all I know, they hoped in and drove off while Black was down there trying to eat me.

"Thank you for telling me," Tad said.

101

"Like I said, I never told you anything," Kyle reminded him. "I'll deny it."

"Thank you, regardless," Tad said.

A few minutes later Trooper Miles dropped Rollins off at the scene. He exchanged a few words with Kyle, glad to see him on his feet, and then turned and headed back towards Wickliffe. As soon as he was gone Rollins and Tad met behind the Pine Grove cruiser that had brought them to Ballard County.

"Learn anything?" Tad asked.

"Nothing really," Rollins said. "Shelley's grandmother seemed like a nice little old lady. She said he drove a truck for the family business. Made a run from Washington State to Pine Grove once a week. Then he would come home for a few days and start all over again."

"No enemies? Nobody that would want him dead?"

"He was apparently a regular pillar of the community," Rollins said. "But I'll tell you one thing, that family was loaded. Huge mansion on a hill overlooking the river. Kind of a creepy place with wolf statues all over the yard."

"Wolves?" Tad asked. His mind was running back over what Trooper Kyle had said, and there was no doubt in his mind that he couldn't repeat it.

"Yeah, creepy things," the other man told him. "Just these giant wolves standing around everywhere guarding the place."

He still didn't really believe the story about werewolves, but there was definitely some connection. Four crimes scenes with giant dog or wolf prints and one victim's yard being filled with concrete statues of giant wolves had to be more than a coincidence. He tried

102

to find a logical way to explain it to his friend, but he couldn't.

"You ready to get home?" Rollins asked.

"I don't think so," Tad said. "If you don't care, drop me off in Paducah. I think I am going to stick around for a couple of days."

"Really?"

"Yeah, I'll keep you in the loop."

Owen's pack checked into a rundown motel on a backstreet of Paducah. It was the type of establishment that looked like it charged either long term 'residential' rates or by the hour. It was the type of place where Chloe would have once been concerned for her own safety, but as she stood in front of the bathroom mirror, she realized that her own safety wasn't really in jeopardy. She had become a monster, and had nothing to fear from any low life drug dealer or rapist that might hang out in a place like this.

"You almost done in there?" Dave asked, pounding on the door.

"Shut up," she snapped back.

She ran her fingers down one side of her face. She still looked normal. It was still the same face she had seen in the mirror her entire life, but she knew without a doubt that she was no longer the same person. She had killed a man earlier that day. She had walked up behind him and ripped his heart out, and as he laid there dead, she'd eaten it.

Chloe wanted that thought to make her sick to her stomach, but it didn't. She didn't feel anything about it. Killing him meant nothing more to her than smashing a bug under her shoe.

"Hurry it up, I need to go!" Dave yelled, resuming his pounding on the door.

In the mirror she saw her eyes as they suddenly flashed red. In the blink of an eye her teeth grew into sharpened fangs. She whirled and threw the bathroom door open, driving herself into Dave's chest. They flew backwards, crashing through a wooden desk chair and turning over the antique mini-fridge.

"Hey, hey, hey, calm it down!" Dave pleaded.

Chloe slashed him across the chest with her hand, ripping four deep gashes into his bare chest with her claws. He cried out in pain, and his own eyes lit up. Before he could react she started punching him in the face, crushing his nose and busting his lip open.

"Enough!" Owen yelled. "Break it up."

She looked up at the alpha, who was laying on one of the room's two beds and growled. She wanted to kill him. Chloe wanted to leap on top of Owen and rip his throat out with her teeth. Then she would pull his heart out of his chest and eat it. That would make her feel better. That would make her happy.

"Change back, girl," the alpha ordered and she felt herself turning back into her fully human form against her will.

Chapter Fifteen

"As you might imagine, tracking another were-wolf is not all that hard," Miles explained. "The hard part is tracking him without him knowing you're tracking him. Once you get close, he will be able to catch your scent as well as you can smell his."

Steve had joined Miles and four other members of Elizabeth's pack in a large clearing surrounded on all sides by trees. The place clearly had some ceremonial significance to the pack. A large fire pit stood at the center of the clearing, and was surrounded by a series of concrete benches arranged in a circular pattern. But all of that was behind them. Their little group was gathered at the edge of the clearing near the mouth of a trail head.

"We're all experienced at this, so I'm just doing this for you, Steve," Miles said to him. "There are a number of methods by which you can try to mask your scent from other werewolves, but there is only one that is fool proof. Follow me."

Miles started down the trail. Despite the darkness he didn't produce a flashlight, and Steve was surprised to find that he didn't need one. He could see almost perfectly in the darkness.

They had followed the trail a hundred or so feet into the forest when suddenly he was struck by a sickeningly sweet odor. It made his eyes water and he had to hold back the urge to regurgitate. As the smell surrounded him he could sense another odor hidden deep below it that would have fallen somewhere between the garbage bin behind a Mexican restaurant and a rotting corpse.

"What is that?"

"Common wolf's bane," the other man said. "Quite possibly the worst thing a werewolf will ever smell. Legends give it all kinds of supernatural qualities, but the truth is, it just smells really bad."

"And we're going to use it?"

"Oh yeah," the other man said. "Take a whiff. I'm standing two feet away from you and you wont be able to smell me."

Steve tried, and Miles was right. The horrible smell of the wolf's bane entirely masked the werewolf's scent. It also caused him to gag and nearly vomit on the other man's shoes, which made the big trooper start laughing.

"Just a little FYI, wolf's bane is toxic," he said. "It'll just make you or me sick if we ate it, but you want to make sure you take a shower before you pick up your little girl."

"What exactly are we going to do with it?"

"We're going to cover ourselves in it."

"But if it blocks our scent, how are we going to track them?" Steve asked.

"A lycan's sense of smell is a lot stronger than that of a human," Miles said. "It masks the scent, it doesn't really block it. We will be focused on one or two specific scents. It's kinda like being able to identify a planet in the night sky. If you know what you're looking for, it's pretty easy. If you don't, it just blends in with the stars."

Fifteen minutes later the search party had gathered back in the clearing. They were stripped down and had their bodies covered with wolf's bane flowers. Miles had given them all empty canvas sacks for their clothes and other belongings, telling them to carry the sacks in their mouths when they ran.

Each man knew that Elizabeth had passed down the order that Owen's pack was to be taken alive. They also knew that Dave and Chloe were expendable. They were half breeds. Owen came from a line of werewolves, so someone out there might actually care whether he

106

lived or died.

The thought brought Steve's anger to the surface, which triggered the start of his change. The rest of the little search party seemed to take that as a sign and they all started the change. Miles was the first to morph into his wolf form. His change happened almost instantly. In less than thirty seconds the six men that had been standing in the clearing had been replaced by five werewolves and Steve, who still hadn't let go of his human half. He was now somewhere between a werewolf and a human. If he could see himself he would have thought he looked like 'the Wolfman' from the old black and white film.

Miles rose up on his hind legs and growled at Steve, who could sense what the other werewolf wanted. He wanted him to complete the change. But he was resisting. He could feel the wolf trying to get out, and he was afraid of letting it take over. He was afraid that once he did, there would be no going back. Soon the rest of the pack, impatient to get on the trail, started growling along with their leader.

At last he decided that he had no choice. Steve let go and felt the beast step forward. He felt his limbs stretch and bend unnaturally. He had thought his eye site had been amazing when he had walked into the dark woods, but suddenly everything was almost as bright as if the sun had decided to reverse it's course and pop back up over the horizon. At the same time he felt a strange power building up inside himself. It was a combination of strength and energy that was unlike anything he had ever known. He wanted to run. He needed to run. And he felt like once he started, he could run forever.

When Miles was satisfied with his transformation, he barked. Steve's wolf ears heard the sound and translated, "Follow."

The pack started running, following in line behind the giant wolf that had been a state trooper only a moment before. They followed a path through the woods, coming out on a deserted stretch of gravel road, which they crossed without a second thought. The group then charged into the forest on the far side, skirting the fence row of a farmhouse where a terrified dog barked at them as they passed.

They moved at speeds which Steve couldn't have imagined, and he had no problem keeping up. Soon they emerged from the forest in sight of Highway 62. There were still a collection of emergency vehicles gathered around the spot where his truck had broken down. But in the blink of an eye they were gone and the pack was entering another stretch of forest.

Steve could smell the werewolf they were after. But more importantly, now he could smell his wife.

"What are we going to do now?" Dave asked. He was still glaring at Chloe, but the gash marks on his chest had mostly healed over. He was laying on one bed while Owen remained on the other. Chloe had taken up residence in the floor near the back of the room.

"He has to die," Owen said.

"Will they give him to us?"

"No, Elizabeth Shelley will protect him as long as he is in her territory. But he wont be there long. They wont let him stay through the full moon. Tomorrow or the next day he'll continue west, and we will be there to greet him."

"I can't wait to take care of this so we can get back on the road," Dave said.

Owen didn't respond. He was thinking about how much he was going to enjoy ripping the other werewolf's throat out. He needed a fresh start. When he had left the tribe to go out on his own, his father and the other elders

108

had cautioned him about who he chose to allow into his pack. He hadn't listened, which was pretty much the story of his life. He'd always had a problem with authority, which had led to trouble with the tribe elders on several occasions. That was what had eventually brought about his voluntary expulsion from the Lakota pack.

They had never really kicked him out, but Agleska had suggested he might be happier if he went out on his own. Even at the time Owen had known that it was the alpha's way of being rid of him, but it hadn't mattered. They were offering him freedom from the rigorous guidelines of the Lakota pack and he was happy to take it.

"Where we going to go next?"

"Haven't really thought much about it," Owen said. "There's another independent pack down in Florida. Spending some time on the beach might be good for a change. Lot's of drunken college students down there, and nobody is ever really surprised when a few of them go missing."

"I'd love to have me a hot college chick," Dave mused. "You think that pack would mind a few visitors?"

"Nah, we're cool."

Owen knew of a half dozen packs like his own, all headed by werewolves whose packs had thought they would be better off without them. They weren't all that social with the old packs, but they all went out of their way to be friendly to each other. Since the council had decided that they could only have four members, their strength was limited. For a long time he had been considering what kind of power those packs could have if they ever banded together. With their forces pulled together and with a strong man leading them, the independent packs could tell the council where to stick their regulations.

"What about *her*?" Dave asked.

"She's my new prized pupil, Davey," he said, grinning at her. Chloe growled at him. "I think I might keep her around and make her my mate. I bet she could give me some real good pups."

"Bite me," she snapped.

"I already have, darlin'," he laughed. "Once the full moon get's here, I bet you calm down a little. You'd best forget about your husband and little girl anyhow, because they are as good as dead. Be nice to me and I wont even make you watch them die. How about that?"

Suddenly the smell of rotting garbage filled his senses. The first thought he had was that they really had to get rid of Charles' body, and then the front wall of their hotel room seemed to explode inward.

Chapter Sixteen

They followed the trail to a small dive hotel. Owen's truck was parked a few blocks away, on a dark and mostly deserted side street. The smell of death came drifting to them, and Miles led the pack over to investigate. For a second Steve was terrified that Owen had killed Chloe, but when they circled around the truck, he saw that the corpse belonged to a dead male werewolf. He recognized the dirty work he had done to the guy back at his father's house.

"Follow," Miles barked again.

They moved quickly and stealthily through a neighborhood, crossing backyards as dogs barked at them and cat's ran in terror. By the time the homeowners could get up to look outside, the pack was already gone. Finally they emerged at the back of a parking lot for the hotel.

"Down," their leader barked.

The six werewolves dropped down onto their haunches as a delivery truck rambled slowly by. Steve could smell the man's coffee and the whiskey that he had poured into it before leaving home. He also caught a whiff of three cats, which he assumed lived inside the guy's house. Then the truck turned a corner and was gone.

The motel was mostly deserted. There were a few rusted out old beaters parked near the front of the lot, but otherwise the place did not seem to be doing much business. His nose could smell a dozen or so people in the place, many of them stinking of body odor and drugs. Mingled in with those odors he could also pick up the three werewolves they were looking for.

Miles dropped his sack and changed back into his human form. He grabbed his cellphone and made a call. Steve could hear the phone ringing on the other end, and he could hear Elizabeth when she picked up on the other end.

"We've found them," Miles told her. "Olney Motor Lodge back parking lot."

"I'll send the truck," she said and hung up.

"Remember, Aunt Liz wants them all alive if possible," he told the group. Then his eyes began to glow and he quickly changed back into his wolf form.

The werewolves crossed the motel parking lot slowly. Miles was in the lead, his nose to the ground. He tracked Owen's pack to a flight of stairs that lead up to the second floor, and then almost to the end of the corridor. The pack gathered at the room next to theirs, barely able to fit onto the second story platform.

"She's my new prized pupil, Davey," Steve heard Owen say. A clearly female growl came back at him. "I think I might keep her around and make her my mate. I bet she could give me some real good pups."

"Bite me," she snapped.

"I already have, darlin'," Owen laughed. "Once the full moon get's here, I bet you calm down a little. You'd best forget about your husband and little girl anyhow, because they are as good as dead. Be nice to me and I wont even make you watch them die. How about that?"

Hearing the other man talk that way to his wife and about his daughter, pushed Steve over the edge. What little grip he still had on his human self was gone, and the wolf came all the way to the surface. He drove forward through the pack and straight at the motel room's front window. Without hesitation he dove through. The widow exploded in a shower of glass and plaster.

His feet landed on the dirty carpet between two beds. Owen was on one and Dave was on the other. Both

112

men rose, changing as they moved. Dave was bigger and faster, thus the more immediate threat. Steve caught him by the throat in mid-change. He sank his claws into the still partially human flesh and drove the man's body backwards hard enough that they both smashed through the wall into the adjoining room, which luckily was empty.

Dave growled and clawed at his arms, but Steve didn't let up. He drove his other clawed hand into the bigger man's stomach, slicing and tearing as he went.

They landed on a bed and flipped over onto the floor.

"Get...off...me," Dave growled.

Steve clamped his jaws down on the other wolf's throat and tore, ripping out Dave's jugular and windpipe.

Dave's arms flailed at him for a moment, and then seemed to go limp. His body began to spasm as blood gurgled out of his open throat. Then his eyes unfocused and he was still. As Steve watched, his body slowly began to transform back into it's human form.

He spun and dove back through the opening into the other room. Three wolves, including Miles Smith, were struggling to subdue Owen, who was putting up a fight. Steve had every intention of killing him too, until he saw that the remaining wolves had Chloe cornered. She had managed to wedge herself under the sink. They could get to her, but not before she could do some damage of her own. She was still only partially changed and was growling angrily at them. If they tried to approach her she swung her claws at them.

Steve barked at the others, ordering them to step back, but they ignored him.

He stepped between them, planning to protect his wife but one of the wolves latched onto his arm. Steve howled in pain and dove on the wolf. The rolled backwards into the dresser, knocking the old television to the floor. For a moment that wolf's companion seemed to forget about Chloe and turned to help his friend.

Chloe dove out from under the sink, her claws flying.

"STOP!" a voice boomed. For a second everything did.

Elizabeth stood in the doorway of the little hotel room, looking horribly out of place in an expensive business suit with a chain of pearls around her neck. Her own pack members lowered themselves like subjects bowing before a queen, while only Steve and Chloe stood and turned to face her.

"Very good," she said. "Take Mr. Black and the girl and place them in the truck. It's waiting at the bottom of the steps."

Several of the wolves grabbed Owen and wrestled him off the bed. He seemed to have gotten over the initial shock of Elizabeth's appearance, but now they had him over powered. Three members of the pack dragged him through the shattered front window and then leapt over the railing with him in their grasp.

Miles and another wolf made a grab for Chloe but Steve jumped between them. He bared his teeth and growled. Before the other two could attack, their alpha stepped forward, placing a hand on each of their backs. The two creatures seemed to shiver and bowed their heads at her touch.

"Be smart, Steve," Elizabeth said. "I know you love your wife, but you wont get out of this room if you put up a fight. Even if you could take out Miles and Eric, there are a half dozen other members of my pack downstairs at the truck. Think about your daughter. She is at

114

my house waiting for you to come back. What happens if you die here?"

Steve stood his ground, but knew what she was saying was true. He had to think about Miranda. If he died, he had no idea what would happen to her. He didn't think Elizabeth would kill her, which meant she would either abandon her or turn her into a member of her pack. He couldn't stand to let either happen. He also couldn't stand to see Miles and his friend attack Chloe in front of him.

He kept eye contact with the old woman as he transformed back into his human form. When he was fully himself again, he reached down and pulled his clothes from the sack he'd carried with him through the woods. He'd dropped it when the fight had started, but he knew right where it had ended up. He dressed himself, aware that every eye in the room was on him, and then took Chloe by the arm.

"I will take her down myself," he said. "She's innocent in all of this, and I wont have one of your people hurting her because of some family feud with Owen Black and his pack."

Steve held Chloe against his chest as they rode back to Elizabeth's house in the back of the delivery truck. The rest of the pack, which had Owen pinned to the floor, watched the two of them with suspicious eyes. The matriarch of the family simply sat stoically on a wooden bench and stared at the rear door as if she had no cares in the world.

"Are they going to kill me?" Chloe asked softly.

"Elizabeth is our friend, I'm sure we will get this sorted out soon," he told her. He wrapped his arm around her shoulders and pulled her closer.

"How's Mir?" she asked for the hundreth time.

115

"Sleeping soundly when I left," he told her. "She will be excited to see you."

"Steve, I don't know...the last time she saw me I tried to kill her."

"That wasn't you, and I think she knows that," he said. "Anyway, I promised her that I would bring you back to her, so I have to."

"She is so small to have to deal with all of this."

"It's probably easier on her than it is us," Steve said. "Kids bounce back pretty quick. Me...I still haven't come to terms with this yet. How is any of this even possible? It goes against everything we've learned since we were in diapers."

"How...how do you resist?" Chloe asked.

"I don't know. I really don't."

"God, I'm a horrible mother," she said, tears starting to stream down her cheeks. "I was going to kill her. I didn't want to, but I was going to because he told me to do it. How could I do that? I'm a horrible...horrible mother, Steve. You should have let them kill me."

"Don't feel bad, it has nothing to do with what kind of person you are, and everything to do with what kind of wolf you are," Elizabeth said. "It's not something we learn, it's a trait we either have or we don't. Most don't. Most of our kind will live their entire life and never disobey a direct order from the leader of their pack."

"Are you going to kill me?" Chloe asked, weakly.

"That will not be up to me," the other woman said, remaining emotionless. "I have already contacted the council of elders. They will arrive the day following the full moon. They have their ways of finding out the truth. If you had nothing to do with my grandson's death, then you will survivie."

116

Chapter Seventeen

Steve hadn't known what kind of arrival to expect once they reached Elizabeth's house, but it definitely was not the kind he and Miranda had received. At least twenty werewolves lined the driveway, all of them showing at least some variation of the change. Some looked like humans with glowing eyes and sharp teeth, while others had taken on a vague wolfish outline. They all growled and snarled at Owen and Chloe as they stepped down from the delivery truck.

He pulled his wife closer, ready to defend her if he had to. He felt no fear for his own safety, only a soul wrenching desire to protect his family. In that moment he had no doubt he could have taken out a few of them before they managed to kill him.

With Elizabeth taking the lead and the hunters dragging Owen in their midst, the little group started up the walk, right through the middle of the rabid crowd. Teeth were bared and a few stray claws swung at them, but no blows landed. That was all it would have taken to push him over the edge, and he knew it. Perhaps they did as well, because the crowd seemed to keep just enough control to not start a war.

Instead of going into the house, the group turned towards a building situated at the rear of the house. Marvin stood solemnly beside the structure's front door, his arms folded stiffly across his chest. Even from fifty feet away, Steve could smell the man's fear. It was a mixture of sweat and a faintly sour odor. Although familiar with his employer's secret, the man clearly was not comfortable being around when the pack was on the verge of a riot.

When the group was close, Marvin opened the building's door to reveal a large silver gate. He shoved an old metal key into the keyhole and undid the lock.

The gate opened to reveal a large room filed with several silver barred cells. The faint scent of old body odor and human waste drifted up to his nose.

"This is not the first time we've needed to restrain members of the lycan community," Elizabeth said to him. "You can trust that your wife will be well cared for while in our custody, Mr. Slate."

"Why do you have to lock her up?" he protested. "You've got your rogue werewolf. She's not going to hurt anyone now."

"Neither of us know what she is going to do, Steve. She probably doesn't even know herself. And she wouldn't exactly be safe roaming around with the rest of my pack swearing a blood oath against who ever killed my poor grandson. She stays here and she stays alive."

"Then at least let her see our daughter before you lock her up!"

The older woman stared curiously at him for a moment. He expected her to say no, but he saw a strange look in her eyes. For all of her fierceness, he sensed a very strong human side to her. The side that was ready to punish Owen not for killing a member of her pack, but because he had killed a member of her family. He should have realized it sooner, after seeing the way her grandchildren were treated, but he'd missed it.

"I will give you fifteen minutes, no more," she said. "Marvin will escort you to your room, and he will be sure that you are undisturbed. Then she will come back here and be locked up as far from the leader of her pack as possible."

Miranda was still sleeping soundly when they slipped into the bedroom. He flipped on the bedside lamp, having to remind himself that although he could see in the dark now, she was still mortal. She wouldn't

118

have been able to see them in the dark.

Finally alone, Chloe turned to him and kissed him tenderly. He wrapped his arms around her and pulled her to him. A soft sob escaped his wife before she fought to control herself. She buried her face in his shoulder and he held onto her. He had no words of comfort. He could find nothing fitting to say in a situation like this, so he simply held on. After a moment she pulled away and stood facing him.

"I'm the one who killed her grandson," she said, and Steve felt like he had been punched in the stomach. "Owen ordered me to protect him, so I did."

"They have to understand that," he said. "You had no choice."

"You heard them, Steve, they are going to find out who did it and punish them," Chloe told him. "They are going to kill me the day after the full moon."

"It's not going to happen," Steve promised her. "If I have to kill everyone here, they are not going to punish you for a crime you did not willingly commit."

"But they will."

He pulled her back to him, once again at a loss for words. But he knew then that he would have to do something. He had gotten her back, he was not going to lose her again.

"Let me see my daughter," she said, pulling away.

Steve stood back as Chloe sat down on the edge of the bed. For a moment she stared at Miranda's angelic face as she lay sleeping, her hands folded together as if in prayer. She leaned down and kissed the little girl on the forehead, and her eyes fluttered open.

"Mommy?" Miranda asked weakly. Then she smiled and her whole face lit up. She leapt up and threw her arms around her mothers neck as if she had no mem-

119

ory of what had happened at Owen's house. "Mommy!"

"Hey baby, how are you?" Chloe asked, tears welling up in her eyes.

"I love you mommy."

Steve turned his back and felt the wolf creeping into him. He couldn't say that he had ever hated anyone in his entire life, but he knew hatred now. He hated Owen Black with every inch of his being, both human and werewolf. He wanted the man dead, but he didn't want the pack of elders to do it. He wanted to do it himself. He wanted to rip the man limb from limb while listening to him screaming.

The sound of Miranda laughing brought him back. He turned around in time to see Chloe tucking her back into bed and promising to be home soon. He knew it was a lie, and that made his hatred even stronger. But he maintained control for his girls' sake.

A moment later there was a knocking on the door and he knew that Marvin was ready to take his wife to her silver prison in the backyard.

"I will get you out of this," he said to her.

"I love you."

Marvin pushed the door open but stepped back as Elizabeth stepped quietly into the room. Her face was once again emotionless as she dangled the keys to his truck in front of her.

"Mr. Slate, I think it will be best if you leave us in the morning," she said.

Miles Smith had already taken control of the crime scene at the Daylight Motor Lodge when Tad Tuttle guided his rental car into a parking spot. Tad noted Owen Black's vehicle as soon as he stepped out into the cool night air. The vehicle was surrounded and a state police crime scene unit was working in the back.

"Good morning, Detective Tuttle," Smith said from the upper level of the motel. He was sipping coffee from a Styrofoam coffee cup.

"I heard on the scanner that you've got two bodies?"

"That's affirmative," the trooper said. "One in the truck and one in what's left of the room."

"Hopefully not Slate and his daughter."

"No," Smith said, but a strange look passed over his face. Once again Tad had the feeling that the man knew more about this case than he was telling. "Looks like two associates of Owen Black, but Mr. Black himself is not present."

Tad glanced towards the truck where CSI's were dragging a corpse into a body bag. When the body appeared to be secure, one of the men reached down and picked up a head, which he placed in the bag along with the rest of the body.

"Coroner estimates that he's been dead about thirty-six hours," Smith told him. "Looks like he was shot a few hundred times and then he was decapitated."

"That could be my missing body," Tad said. "The state police lab in Madisonville will be able to confirm DNA."

"You get that Tommy?" the trooper yelled down to the crime scene guys, one of which waved back. "Now, feel free to look around my crime scene all you want, Detective, but consider this my case now."

"But that's my body."

"I put in a call, the KSP will be handling your investigation as well," Smith said. He smiled apologetically. "I'm not trying to play big brother here. I called your department trying to reach you, but since you were out of town they transferred me to your chief. He said Miltonboro doesn't have the manpower to handle this,

121

and requested that the state police take over. I humbly accepted."

Tad stared at him. It wasn't his first time losing a case to the Kentucky State Police. His little police department really didn't have the manpower or the resources to work this case, but that didn't make it sting any less. It was a fairly common practice for the state boys to take lead in a murder cases. Now that they had a body, this was most certainly a murder case.

"Who is in the room?" he asked at last.

"ID on the dresser says David Fischer, a resident of Souix Falls, South Dakota," Smith said. "Small time crook. Record of convictions for drug possession. He's listed as an employee of a construction company owned by Owen Black, but as best I can find, that company hasn't done much work for several years."

"From what I've seen they've been demolishing a lot of buildings," Tad said, looking at the shattered front wall of the motel room. "No sign of Black or the Slate family?"

"In the wind."

Chapter Eighteen

After buckling Miranda in her car seat, Steve met Elizabeth near the back of the truck. He had been awake all night trying to find the words to say. When he'd found Chloe he had entertained the idea that their family would be whole again, but all of that had changed when she'd confessed that she was the one who had killed Elizabeth's grandson. The older woman seemed convinced that her elders would be able to find out the truth, and she seemed determined to kill the guilty party.

"Don't do this, Elizabeth," he pleaded softly. "My wife is innocent. Owen Black changed her and has had complete control of her ever since."

"We have our ways, Mr. Slate," she said.

"Just let her go with me," Steve suggested. "We will leave here and never come back. You can punish Owen as much as you want. He's not going anywhere. Just let me take my wife and go."

"The council of elders will meet tomorrow night, and they will determine who killed Wayne. That person will be held accountable," Elizabeth told him. "If your wife is found to be guilty, then you have my condolences. If not, she will be free to go."

They stared into each other's eyes, and Steve knew they had come to a breaking point. He could feel the anger building up inside of him. The wolf was growling deep in his soul, waiting for a chance to get out, and Steve wanted to let him out. Despite everything Elizabeth and her pack had done for he and Miranda, he suddenly hated them. They were going to take his wife away from him, and for that he wanted to see them all dead.

"Elizabeth, I appreciate everything you have done for me and my daughter," he said. "I would like to count you as a friend, but if I leave here without my wife, that bridge is burned. I will be back. Until the day that I

123

die, I will make your life a living hell."

"You would threaten me?" she asked in surprise. "After everything I've done for you? Here in the midst of my pack, you would threaten me?"

"I just did," he said softly.

"Go before I change my mind," she said, turning her back on him. As an after thought she turned her head and called back to him. "The next time I see you I will kill you for this."

Steve stood and watched her go. It wasn't the first time he had alienated someone, but she was probably the most dangerous one on the list.

He climbed into the cab of his dad's old pickup, where Miranda was playing with a toy Allison had given her. He ruffled her hair as he started the engine. He put on a smile, although happiness was far from what he was feeling inside.

"Why isn't mommy coming with us?" she asked.

"Mommy has to stay and help Ms. Elizabeth with something," he lied. "I'm going to take you to Uncle Rick's house, and then I'm going to come back and pick her up."

Following Detective Rollins' directions, Tad Tuttle drove from Paducah to the house where Wayne Shelley's family lived on the outskirts of Wickliffe. By the time he drove passed at seven in the morning, the house was already bustling with activity. He counted a few dozen people moving about the property, but mostly around an outbuilding near the back of the house. By the time he turned around and came back, he saw the old Ford pickup truck that belonged to Steve Slate's dad sitting by the front of the house. A small group had gathered to watch as a man loaded a small child into the passenger side of the vehicle.

As he drove back towards town he unfolded the map he had picked up at a truck stop and found his current location. If Slate was making a run for it, he could only see two options. One was to go back the way he had come; the other was to head to the state line which was only a few miles west. The latter seemed most likely.

He turned his rental car towards the Mississippi River and tried to decide how he was going to handle this. Clearly he could not contact the State Police. The case belonged to Smith who was connected with Shelley and his family. Officially he wasn't really even on the case anymore. He was supposed to be heading back to Miltonboro, but he couldn't bring himself to give up yet.

Tad had to know what was going on. After speaking with Smith at the motel, he had walked the parameter, once again noticing the same large dog tracks he had seen at every crime scene. There had been no evidence that the Slates had kept any large animals, either at their house or at the property belonging to Slate's father.

He pulled his cellphone from his jacket pocket and dialed Todd Maxwell. After three rings the coroner picked up.

"Max, you get anything on those hairs we found?" he asked.

"Yeah, the report was in the fax machine when I came in this morning," the other man said. Tad could hear him shuffling through papers. "You owe me big time for this, I had to call in all of the favors I had at the crime lab to get this pushed through."

"That's fine, Max, just tell me what it says."

"Okay, it says here we are dealing with an unknown species of Canis lupus," Max read from the report. "In laymen's terms that's a wolf."

125

"A wolf?" Tad asked. "In Miltonboro?"

"It would appear," the coroner said. "I did a little digging but really didn't come up with much. There is not a particular subspecies for this type of wolf, but traces of them have been found across the globe. It does appear that they are a peculiarly vicious species. Reports show them being suspected in hundreds if not thousands of cases of attacks on humans."

"There has got to be something else going on that we don't know," Tad mused. "Any chance we stumbled upon some kind of illicit dog fighting ring?"

"Your guess is as good as mine," the vet said. "But since you asked, there are 39 known subspecies of Canis lupus. That includes the dingo and the domestic dog."

"You know way too much about dogs, Max."

"I know nothing about dogs, Tad, I simply Googled it and up popped the answer."

"Okay, thanks Max."

Steve was running the clock in his head. It was seven-thirty by the time he pulled out of Elizabeth's driveway, and it a little over four hours to get to Rick's house. That would mean he should arrive around noon. Sunset was around five. From there he would have about twenty four hours until the full moon.

When the time came to face the full moon he wanted to be as far from Rick's house as possible. He didn't want to risk finding his way back to them after he changed. He wouldn't be able to live with himself if he hurt one of them.

Distracted, he didn't see the car pull out in front of him until it was almost too late. Steve locked up the old truck's breaks and slid sideways as the other vehicle came to a dead stop in the middle of the road. He managed to regain enough traction at the last second to drive the truck into a ditch and back up on the other side instead of slamming Miranda's side of the truck into the side of the car.

They came to rest on a dirt embankment a few feet off the highway. The car that cut him off made a u-turn and turned into a pull off just a few feet in front of them.

"You okay, baby?" he asked, checking Miranda over for any sign of injury.

"Daddy, you wrecked the truck," his daughter said, giving him a disapproving look.

"The truck is okay, I just need to make sure you are too," he said. After a brief appraisal he was satisfied that she wasn't hurt.

"Who is that man?" she asked, pointing.

"It's not polite to point, baby," Steve said. He looked in the direction she was pointing and his heart sank. He recognized "Tiny" Tad Tuttle instantly. MPD's lone detective was wearing his chrome shades and had his badge displayed proudly on his belt, along with his handgun. "That man, darling, is a cop from Miltonboro."

"Is he here to get the monster?"

"He might be, darlin', he might be," Steve told her. "You stay here while I talk to him."

He took a deep breath and climbed out of the truck.

"Howdie Tad," he said.

"Steve," the other man said with a nod. He had not drawn his weapon, but his hand hovered around it's vicinity. "There are some things I need you to explain."

"I never thought you'd be the one to find me," Steve said thoughtfully. "Didn't your jurisdiction end about four counties back that way?"

"Something like that," Tad replied. "Look, I've been on this case since we investigated the fire at your father's house."

"Dad's house burned?"

"You didn't know that?"

"Had no idea. Did you find anything?"

"A lot of blood and a lot of animal fur," Tad said. "Wolf hair, to be more specific."

"A wolf in Miltonboro?" Steve asked, taken aback. Through everything that had happened, he had yet to consider what he was going to say to the police if they caught up with him. "That seems highly unlikely."

"I thought so too, but lab tests confirmed it," the detective said. He paused, looking from Steve to Miranda, who was playing with her toys in the truck. "I can help you, Steve. If you've gotten mixed up in something, I can help. I don't think you have anything to do with what's going on. I think you are an innocent party that somehow got caught up with some bad people. If you'll tell me what's going on, I promise to help you."

Steve was touched. He and Tad Tuttle didn't really know each other. They were two guys who played baseball together fifteen years ago and shared a couple of classes in high school. They hadn't said two words to each other since, and if this hadn't happened, they probably wouldn't have said two more words to each other the rest of their lives. But here they were.

"I can't explain what is going on," Steve said after a brief hesitation. "I don't have time, and you probably wouldn't believe me even if I did. What I can tell you is that my wife is in danger, and if I don't get my daughter to a safe place by nightfall, she will be too."

"You can trust me," Tad told him.

"It's not a matter of trust, Tad. I was targeted by

some bad people for no other reason other than they lived next door to me. I was supposed to die two days ago, but things didn't work out for them. Because of it my wife's life is now in danger. I have to get my daughter to safety and then try to get my wife back."

"Does Owen Black have your wife?"

"Man, just let me go," Steve pleaded. "They're going to kill her in two days if I don't save her."

"Why don't we save her together?" Tad asked.

Tad studied Slate's eyes as they talked, trying to see any sign that the man was telling a lie. He saw nothing. There was no hint that the other man was misleading him, just the pure panic of a man who was trying to save his family from some unknown disaster. He felt a little sympathy for him. Sometimes bad things happen edto good people, and this could very well be one of those times.

But what could he do? As Steve had said, he was well out of his jurisdiction. It also wasn't his case anymore, not since the State Police took it over. He didn't even have the authority to be here asking questions. Yet, here he was, and he found himself wanting to help. He didn't know if it was part of his subconscious wanting to help out an old teammate, or if there was something to this case that just rubbed him the wrong way.

"Tell me what's going on and I will help you, you have my word," he promised. "I don't have the authority here to stop you, but I can call the state police before you have time to get back in your truck. They'll make a call and the Missouri State Police will meet you on the other side of the river."

"Okay, fine," Steve said with a sigh. "Do you believe in the supernatural?"

"You mean like ghosts?"

"You worked the second Peppermint Man case, didn't you?"

"Yeah."

"There were lots of rumors that said you guys uncovered evidence that Billy Jones was possessed," Steve said. "Do you believe any of that? Do you believe that there are things out there that can't be explained by modern science?"

Tad stared at him for a moment. The Billy Jones case had been the biggest of his career, and he hadn't even been a detective then. He had been a local patrolman assigned to work with the state trooper who eventually shot and killed Billy Jones, the son of the infamous serial killer known as "The Peppermint Man". In the aftermath they had found a lot of evidence, some of which did seem to hint at either insanity or demonic possession. He had never really believed in such things, but Glenn Wyatt, the trooper who shot Jones, had eventually bought into it.

"I don't know about supernatural, but I think there are things that science cannot explain yet," he answered. "That doesn't mean they will never be able to explain it. Why don't you try me?"

"What do you think about werewolves?"

Chapter Nineteen

Reluctantly, Steve told Tad Tuttle everything, from his ill-fated hunting trip to the capture of Owen Black and Chloe. He watched to see how the other man would react, expecting to see doubt in his eyes. He didn't. Steve was pretty sure the cop didn't believe him about the werewolves, but he believed there was something strange going on.

"You say you have to get your daughter to Arkansas by tomorrow night, right?" Tad asked.

"Yeah."

"Give me twenty-four hours. Tonight I will stop by that house and have a look in the barn. If I see your wife and Owen Black locked up in cages, I'll contact the FBI, the CIA or Homeland Security. Anything you want."

"You'll never get on the property," Steve told him. "They will smell you coming and you'll be dead before you ever get started."

"You said the wolfsbane covered your scent," Tad offered. "If it will cover up the scent of a werewolf, surely it will cover up the scent of a normal human like myself, right?"

Steve nodded. Although he wanted all the help he could get, he didn't like this. He did not believe for a minute that Tad Tuttle stood a chance against Elizabeth's pack. Even with the wolfsbane. He wished there were some other way to convince Tad that he was telling the truth. He tried to think of anyway around letting the man see him change, but it was the only way. Without seeing it, he didn't see any way that Tad or anyone else would ever believe.

It was the only thing he could think of, and then he didn't know if he could do it. He had never made himself change on purpose. Every time he had given in

131

to the change there had been a trigger, even when he had gone with the pack to locate Owen and Chloe. He had yet to make himself change for the sake of changing. Then there was the fact that, even if he could trigger the change, he was deathly afraid that he wouldn't be able to stop it.

"Follow me," he said, starting off towards Tad's car. The detective followed, looking a little confused. "I really need you to believe me, Tad."

Like it or not, he was going to have to try. His chances of saving his wife on his own were slim, but he'd try it if he had to. If he could get Tad to work with him, that at least would mean another brain and another gun. The odds were still stacked against him, but he was willing to do anything he could to improve those odds.

As they walked, Steve worked to clear his mind of any thought but Owen Black. Hatred was not an emotion he was used to, but in this case it bubbled easily to the surface. The wolf responded, trying to break free, but he held it back. He had to hold it back. He didn't think he was strong enough to control it if it got to the surface, so he held on to his humanity.

"Where are we going, Steve."

The sensation of his eyesight sharpening hit first, followed closely by an increase in hearing. He was aware of Tad's heart beat racing as they moved, and knew that the other man was half expecting him to pull a gun. If he turned he knew he'd find Tad's hand on the butt of his pistol. A sharp pain shot through his jaw as the bone dislodged itself and started to elongate. Then he felt the hair up and down his arms begin to grow.

Steve turned to face Tad Tuttle. The cop stopped in his tracks, his eyes going wide. In surprise he fumbled for his gun.

"It's okay," Steve said, his voice now unfamiliarly deep and gravely. "I wont hurt you. Not now. I'm still in control."

That was half a lie. He was clinging to control with all of his might, but he felt his grip slipping. The wolf, seeing freedom from it's fleshy cage, was fighting to get to the surface. It was wild and hungry. It wanted out nearly as bad as Steve wanted to save his wife.

"You were telling the truth?"

Steve felt his shoulders pop and start to stretch as the bones rearranged themselves and the muscles around them began to grow. His fingers began to swell and his finger nails sharpened into dangerously sharp claws.

He was losing control.

"Steve...are you...okay?"

He closed his eyes and tried to focus, but it didn't do any good. The wolf was almost free. He could feel it taking control of his body. He suddenly knew wasn't going to be able to stop. He was going to change into a werewolf and kill Tad Tuttle right here on the side of the road. When he was done he was going to kill Miranda.

Steve's eyes shot open. Even from twenty feet away his enhanced eyes could clearly make out Miranda playing in the cab of the truck. He started mentally clawing with all of his might, trying to push the wolf back down below. He had not gone through all of this only to end up killing his daughter on the side of the road.

He glanced at his daughter still sitting in the truck and felt the wolf going away.

"This is insane," Tad said. Reluctantly, Steve had followed the detective to a small rundown motel just a few minutes from the banks of the Mississippi. "I just... werewolves? Really?" He sat on one of the twin beds in Steve and Miranda's room, still looking shocked from his experience along the side of the highway. "I saw it...

but I still can't get my mind around it."

"Try being a werewolf," Steve said. "Are you sure this is necessary? I told you, I have to get Miranda to my brothers house before the full moon."

"I need to see this for myself," the other man said. "I'll just drop in tonight and take a look around. I mean, I saw you change...but my mind still can't believe what I saw. You know what I mean?"

"There is a good chance if you try to get on that property, they will catch you and kill you," Steve said. "As long as I still have Miranda with me, there isn't anything I can do to help you."

"I'll be okay," Tad insisted. "Just tell me where the wolfsbane is. I'll cover myself in it and they'll never smell me coming. I might even be able to see a weak spot we can take advantage of."

Steve really didn't think Tad stood a chance, even if he covered his entire body with wolfsbane. This wasn't a barn full of meth-heads he was dealing with, it was a pack of vicious werewolves. Werewolves who were angry and wanted to take revenge on the person who had killed one of their own. The threats he had made towards Elizabeth would only help to fuel the fire. They might not see him as a threat, but he thought they were at least smart enough to be alert just in case he tried to come back.

"Look, just spend the night here," Tad told him. "I'll check it out and come back. Maybe we can even discuss strategy before you leave for Arkansas. I don't understand any of this, but I've dedicated my life to protect and serve the residents of Miltonboro. This Owen Black guy came in and attacked a family of those residents, so I think he needs to pay for that. I'm just doing my job here."

Steve glanced over at Miranda, who had fallen

134

asleep while playing in an old recliner in the corner of the room. Despite everything, her face was tranquil. Her sleep was the pure sleep of innocence, untroubled by the monsters that surrounded them. He longed to feel that himself but knew he'd never feel that again. The best he could hope for was to let her keep her innocence as long as possible.

"I wont hold you to your promise," Steve said after a brief silence. "If you want to get in your car and go, I wont hold it against you. There is a pretty good chance they'll kill us both when we do try to save her. This is my problem, there's no need for you to involve yourself."

"You can drop it, Steve," the other man told him. "Werewolves invade my town and attack my fellow residents. This is my business."

Chapter Twenty

Tad took a deep breath as he climbed behind the wheel of his rental car. He double checked his service nine millimeter, made sure he had a few extra clips tucked into his jacket pocket. Then he bent down and checked his backup weapon in an ankle holster. The snub nosed .50 caliber revolver held five shots, and he had one speed loader in his pocket with the clips for the other gun. In most situations that would have made him feel well enough armed, but he was about to walk into a crowd of werewolves. There was no way to be adequately armed for that situation.

"What are you doing?" he asked himself, staring into his own eyes in the rear view mirror.

When the man in the mirror didn't answer, he shifted the car into drive and pulled out of the dusty gravel parking lot. He wasn't uncomfortable going in alone. As a member of Miltonboro's finest, he had spent most of his career breaking cases on his own. At it's peak in the late 90's MPD had employed ten patrolmen and two detectives. There had been another three or four patrolmen who worked part time schedules. But after the economy went into the tank the force had shrank, dropping back to only five full time patrolman, one detective and another five part timers.

The only backup he ever saw was when he called in the state police or the sheriff's department, which he avoided. Those outside agencies were like stray cats. Once you opened the door they were apt to swoop in and try to take over. He didn't mind giving up the credit, but outsiders tended to not respect the locals as much. A lot of the time arrests went bad when they were on the scene, not because they didn't do their jobs well, but because they approached things differently than someone who lived there.

As he drew near the house, he hoped that Miles Smith was anywhere but Wickliffe. Knowing what he knew now, he didn't think the state trooper was dirty, but the man definitely had a conflict of interest in this case. His family connection to one of the murder victims was the least of it. Considering that the world believed werewolves were a myth, their secret must be something they protected very dearly. It would be something they were willing to kill to protect.

Tad drove by the big house and into the woods. He spotted a pullover near the place where Steve told him he would find the wolfsbane and turned the rental car into the grass. He double checked his firearms and ammo again before stepping out into the cool night air. The moon shone down from above.

Before he could have second thoughts, he plunged into the dark forest. The moon light was bright enough for him to slowly make his way through the trees without falling over a downed tree trunk or root, but it was far from bright. If anything was in here with him, it would see him well before he saw it.

After nearly ten minutes of walking he could see the growing light of a clearing ahead. He slowed his pace even more as he drew close, carefully watching for any sign that someone or something might be lurking beyond the edge of the forest. In the center of the clearing was a giant fire pit surrounded by rows of stone seats. It looked vaguely like an outdoor ampetheater, which made him wonder what kind of monstrous shows werewolves gathered here to watch.

Steve had told him that a trail led from the clearing to the patch of wolfsbane, so he circled around the clearing, just inside the forest's edge. Fifty feet from where he had first arrived he found a trail head. It was narrow, but clearly identifiable. He turned and headed back into the darkness.

Tad emerged back into the clearing several minutes later, wolfsbane draped around his neck. He hoped the stuff worked as good as Steve claimed. If it didn't, he might not know about it until it was too late.

He guessed the old barn was about two hundred yards from the fire pit across mostly open ground. The moon that had helped him find his way through the forest would now reveal his presence to anyone that happened to be looking in his direction. But from what he could see, there wasn't much going on around the place. A few lights burned in upper windows of the house, but the property around it seemed to be deserted.

Stealth assault wasn't a course they taught at the police academy, but he'd learned enough during the years of hunting he'd done as a teen and young adult to keep the sounds of his progress to a minimum. Although he knew it was a pointless gesture, he drew his 9mm and held it at ready, just in case. If he did happen to encounter something, he'd at least like to put a few hollow tips in it before it ripped him apart.

Tad moved slowly from tree to tree, carefully making his way across the yard, trying to keep as much of his movements as possible to the shadows.

He still couldn't really explain to himself what he was doing here. He had watched Steve Slate turn from a man to a monster and back again. If that wasn't enough proof of werewolves, he didn't know what would be. Maybe some skeptical part of him still didn't want to believe what he had saw. It would probably haunt him for the rest of his life. Things like this only existed in bad Hollywood movies, they did not live in plantation style homes in rural western Kentucky.

Tad heard a sound and ducked behind an old oak

tree. A man in bibbed overalls stepped out of the barn, visible for only a moment in the glow of the building's interior lights. A few seconds later a lighter sparked to life and lit the end of a cigarette. When the lighter clicked closed, the faint orange glow of the burning tobacco marked his location.

Tad took a seat, his back against the trunk of the old tree. His heart was racing. He had the momentary urge to turn tail and run, but he pushed the feeling away. He had to know what was really going on in that barn. The more time that passed since seeing Steve's transformation, the less his mind wanted to believe it. He needed to see it again.

He peered around the tree in time to see the smoking man crush his cigarette underfoot and enter the house through a side door. Tad waited, mentally counting off sixty seconds. When the man did not reappear he got slowly to his feet and scanned the clearing. Nothing moved.

The final approach to the barn took him across open ground. The only cover he saw was a large white rock that rose up from the soil about halfway across the clearing. He selected that as a way point, thinking he could take cover behind it and regroup before crossing the final distance to the building. It would block him from anyone looking out from the house, and it would give him a straight shot at the side wall of the building.

Keeping low to the ground, Tad started across the yard. Although he was a big man, he moved with the grace of a runner, dodging nearly unseen obstacles and keeping as quiet as possible. By the time he dropped to the ground behind the big white rock, he was satisfied that he'd gone unnoticed.

As he raised up to take a look over the rock, he realized that it wasn't a rock at all, but a statue. One that gave him a chill. He was staring right into the gaping maw of an oversized wolf, expertly carved out of marble. It's sharp teeth gleamed in the glow of the moon, giving them the appearance of being even sharper than they really were.

Beyond the statue everything was quiet. There was no sign of the cigarette smoking man or anyone else. Even a couple of the lights he'd seen on the upper floor of the house had gone out. Everything seemed absolutely normal, and the logical side of his mind told him that there were no such thing as werewolves and he was trespassing. Another part of him new different. He could almost feel the presence of the creatures.

Tad took a deep breath and ducked out from behind the statue. He moved quickly up a slight rise that led to the back corner of the barn and took cover in the shadows at the back of the building.

He hadn't noticed it from a distance, but once he reached the back of the barn, he could see a small gleaming sphere of light near the end of the building. He crept closer, sticking to the shadows, until he could make out an old knot thole in one of the boards. Light from the interior of the barn shown out on the dark ground.

Tad dropped to one knee and crawled until he was close enough to peer through the hole. Everything Steve had told him became real in a heartbeat. Inside the barn he could see several rolls of shiny sliver bars, which separated the inside of the building into a number of cells. Inside one on the opposite side of the building from where he stood he could see Chloe Slate laying on her back atop a pile of hay.

He was about to call out to her when a bloodshot eye appeared a half inch from his own on the opposite side of the knot thole. In the instant before he jumped

141

back, he could clearly make out a faint animalistic eye shine.

"Come to save the day?" a voice growled. "Or maybe you came to feed the wolves, huh? Why don't you come on in here and see what we can work out?"

Chapter Twenty-One

"Hey, somebody's down there!" Tad heard a voice call out. He cursed under his breath and turned to run. He heard the back door of the house slam closed.

He made no attempt to mask himself on his way back across the clearing. He could hear the running footsteps of at least two men chasing him, quickly closing the distance. He knew his only chance would be to make it into the forest and hope the wolfsbane masked his scent enough for him to reach his car.

Tad was almost to the trail head when a hand reached out to grab him by the shoulder. He tried to lean his upper body forward out of their grasp, but lost his balance and went tumbling forward. He turned the fall into a roll, coming up facing his attackers with his gun ready.

"Stop or I'll shoot," he said. "I'm a police officer."

"Why don't you show us your badge?" one of the men asked. It was the big man in bibbed overalls.

"It's right here on my hip," Tad told him, aiming his hip in their direction.

"Miltonboro?" the man asked. "I don't know where that is, detective, but you don't have any authority out here."

He was amazed that the man had been able to read his badge in the dark, but Tad reminded himself that he was dealing with werewolves. They had abilities he could not fathom, which apparently included the ability to see in the dark.

"What do you want?" bibbed overalls asked.

"Just following up on a lead," Tad explained.

The second werewolf was beginning to pant like a dog. Tad could see his eyes as they transitioned from normal to glowing an amber color. His teeth were starting to sharpen and elongate.

"Jerry, keep it in check, son," the other man warned. "This ain't just some meth addict out looking to score. We can't just kill him and toss him in the river. He's a cop. We need to talk to Miles about this."

"Okay...Robert," Jerry said reluctantly.

"I apologize for my cousin's behavior," Robert said to Tad. "Sir, I'd like to ask you to turn your weapon over and follow us up to the house."

"No, I think I am fine, gentlemen," Tad said. He started to inch backwards towards the edge of the forest. He had come up six feet short. "I'll just be on my way. No need to trouble anybody."

"Sir, you don't understand," Robert said. His eyes started to glow.

"I think I do," Tad said.

Before anything else could be said he shot Robert in the chest from two feet away. The man clutched at the wound and fell to the ground. Jerry growled and lunged at him. Tad shot him twice in the abdomen before turning to run into the forest.

Tad hoped Steve was wrong and the bullets would keep the two men down, but without even turning his head he knew they were both after him. He could hear the sounds of pursuit. It wasn't the sounds a person normally made when they ran. It was a raspy, panting sound. Like a dog.

He charged through the forests, dodging downed logs and tree trunks with an agility he hadn't used since high school baseball. But no matter how fast he ran, he could feel them gaining on him. He resisted the urge to turn and look, because he knew Lot's wife wasn't the only one to meet her end by looking back. He focused every ounce of his attention on where he was going.

Out of the corner of his eye Tad saw movement. He turned his head just enough to see a large black shape charging through the forest on an intersecting path with his own. He couldn't make the shape out, even with the moon light, but he could tell it was much to large and moved way to fast to be human.

At the last possible second he pulled out an old baseball trick and dropped as if he was sliding feet first into home. As the dark, furry shape passed just overtop of him he fired twice into it's belly. It let out a pained yelp and went crashing into the trees.

Tad popped back up, his pursuers now just a few feet away. He could see the highway just a few meters ahead and could hear the sound of a vehicle approaching quickly from the south. He only hoped that the werewolves would not be so bold as to reveal themselves in the middle of a state highway.

As he crashed out of the trees onto the blacktop, he pulled his badge from his belt with his free hand. He held the badge up and pointed his gun at the approaching headlights. They were closer than he had thought, he realized when it was too late to do anything. He closed his eyes and waited as the vehicle's brakes locked up.

Then the only sound was the ticking of the car's engine. He opened his eyes and breathed a sigh of relief. The driver had stopped only inches in front of him.

The driver's door of the vehicle opened and the operator climbed out. Tad squinted against the headlights, trying to make out the driver's face. All he could see was the vague outline of a man, but something about him struck Tad as familiar. Then Miles Smith stepped into the headlights.

"I told you to get on home, Detective," the state trooper said. "What am I supposed to do with you now? You've seen way too much for me to just let you go."

The forest around them seemed to come alive. A few dozen dark shapes emerged from the trees, their eyes glowing red like fire. Tad lowered his weapon and waited for the inevitable.

Steve had planned to stay awake until Tad came back, but at some point during the night he'd drifted off to sleep. When he opened his eyes the first rays of sunlight were peeking through the motel room's blinds. He sighed and pulled Miranda closer to him. If Tad was coming back, he'd have been back well before daylight.

He was on his own again, and time was running out.

PART TWO
The Hunter

Chapter Twenty Two

The flat river land of eastern Missouri gave way to the hilly Ozark region. Steve watched the sky nervously as they chased the sun towards the western horizon. The downside to going to his brother's house was that there was no direct route. No interstate or parkway. The old truck followed two lane roads all the way across 'The Show Me State'.

They stopped at a Burger King near West Plains, MO for lunch early in the afternoon, then headed on towards Norfork Lake. Near the town of Tecumseh, MO traffic ground to a halt. They were only a half dozen miles from Highway J, which would take them into the state of Arkansas, but they were stopped dead.

Steve stared at his watched and waited impatiently for any sign that traffic would be moving again soon. About fifteen minutes later a Missouri state trooper flew by, followed closely by an ambulance. Miranda watched the flashing lights with wonder, then went back to playing with her toys.

He wished he'd thought to buy a GPS while he was in Red's, but it had never occurred to him. Even though he and Rick didn't see each other often, he at least knew the way to his house. The idea that they might come across road construction or an accident had never crossed his mind. He considered pulling out of line and trying some side road, but he was afraid that would put them in an even worse condition than they were already in. At least for the moment he knew where he was.

"I love you very much, baby," he told Miranda as they waited in line.

"I love you more," she said with a grin, looking up from her toys. "And I love you and I love mommy and you both love me!"

149

"That's right," he said. "We both love you very very much. More than I know how to tell you."

Not knowing what else to say, he let her go back to playing and continued his vigil in silence. He was still pretty certain they could make it to Rick's. Whatever was blocking the road had to get cleared at some point, and then they could get moving again. For the first time since all of this started, he felt that Miranda would soon be safe. Maybe it was that moment of relief that allowed the sudden wave of doubt in. For the first time he admitted that he might not make it through tonight.

For the last two days his only concern had been getting Miranda to his brother's. With that one task almost complete, he realized that this might be the end for him. Elizabeth had implied that it was next to impossible for a werewolf to survive their first full moon alone. In just a matter of hours he would have to do just that, if he wanted to have any chance of saving Chloe and seeing Miranda again.

A wave of despair washed over him, and he felt his eyes begin to burn as they filled with tears. But he knew he couldn't let his daughter see him crying, so him wiped the tears away and looked out the side window.

A moment later he saw the first car approaching from the west.

They crossed into Arkansas with no other problems. Rick lived just a few miles outside of the little community of Clarkridge, along the banks of Norfork Lake. Steve figured they were less than five miles away, and he had thirty or forty-five minutes until the full moon should trigger the change.

They were going to make it to Rick's in time, he thought, just before the front driver's side tire of the pickup decided to pop. Steve had the old truck pushed to nearly seventy when he felt the *thump...thump...thump*, followed immediately by the sound of the tire blowing out. There was no time to brake. All he could do was hold on and try to keep from killing them both.

When the tire blew, the front end of the truck pulled hard to the left into oncoming traffic, but he steered hard the other way. The old rubber came off the rim and sparks started to fly as the rim tore into the asphalt.

The truck's remaining front tire went off the shoulder of the road and the old Ford followed, going entirely into a ditch, where it buried itself in the edge of a muddy field, stopping the forward momentum with a jerk. Luckily their speed had slowed enough that the stop wasn't as bad as it could have been. Miranda started crying, but he was pretty sure she had come out of the accident without a scratch.

"It's okay, baby," he said as he snapped her out of her car seat. For a moment he forgot where they were and what was going on. The only thing on his mind was making sure his daughter was okay. He unfastened her seatbelt and pulled her into his arms. "You're okay, I've got you."

"What happened, daddy?" she asked through teary eyes.

"I think we had a flat tire," Steve told her. "There is a spare in the back, though, so it's okay."

He sat her back in her car seat and opened the door. His eyes glanced towards the horizon, where the sun was starting to drop below the tops of the trees. When he stepped out, he stared down at the spot where the front tire had been. About half of the rim was now buried in Arkansas mud. The truck's front bumper was nearly touching the ground.

Steve closed his eyes and focused. He had to act quickly. He reached behind the driver's side of the old bench seat and grabbed the jack. It sank into the muddy ground when he placed it under the bumper, which actually gave it just enough room to fit. He stuck the tire iron into the jack and started pumping, slowly raising the truck.

But the muddy ground and the angle at which the truck was resting was too much. Steve had raised the truck about half the length of the jack when suddenly it shifted sideways. The shaft of the jack snapped and the tire tool slapped him hard enough in the hip to make him cry out in pain.

That was when he first felt it. He'd felt the wolf before, when it had tried to take control, but that had been nothing like this. It wasn't just a feeling or an urge. The wolf was suddenly a full-blown presence inside his body. He could sense what it wanted. The thing wasn't thinking, not the way a person did, but he could feel it's animalistic impulses. It was an animal locked in a cage and it wanted out. It wanted out and it wanted to hunt.

He could suddenly smell the human scent of his daughter from inside the truck, and the creature felt hunger. That made his own stomach growl. Steve was repulsed. He looked up to the sky and saw the full moon hanging there, taunting him. The sun had almost finished it's descent.

"Baby, stay in the truck," Steve called out and started walking into the field. "Lock the doors and get in the floor."

He wanted to do more, but he didn't have the time. He had given it his all and failed. Steve couldn't stay here to protect her and he couldn't get her somewhere safe. The best thing he could do was to get as far from her as he possibly could.

"Come back daddy!" she yelled. "NO!!! Don't leave me!"

152

Tears were starting to flow down his face, and he was glad, at least, that she couldn't see that. He pressed on through the mud as his daughter called out to him, begging him not to leave her alone. It broke his heart, and it concreted his hatred of Owen Black. That man was responsible for making him break his daughter's heart. If there were any way possible, he would make Owen pay.

"Daddy, don't go!"

Steve felt himself stumbling as he moved through the field. In a way it was like trying to walk with his legs asleep. But his legs weren't asleep. The wolf was creeping out, making it's way into every inch of his body. The battle Elizabeth had told him about was starting, and he could feel himself losing. The animal was too strong. It was going to take control of his body and he would be gone.

Somewhere near the center of the field, Steve Slate collapsed to his knees. He could no longer control his legs at all, and he could now feel the change coming over him. This time was different than the others. The change felt more violent, more powerful. As he knelt in the mud staring at his hands, he could see his nails growing into claws and hair springing out all over them.

Then everything seemed to speed up. His body almost seemed to explode into the form of the wolf, ripping through his clothes in the blink of an eye. The wolf, now totally in charge, raised it's snout to the air and howled wildly at the moon.

"Daddy?" a soft voice said from only a few feet away.

The wolf jumped to it's feet with a snarl, whirling on the poor defenseless girl that had followed her father into the middle of the field. Steve was aware of everything going on, but he was totally helpless to stop it. He was a passenger inside the werewolf's body.

"Daddy?" Miranda cried as he stalked towards her, jaws opened to attack.

The wolf growled. She stumbled backwards and then slipped in the mud. She landed on her backside, unable to run.

Chapter Twenty Three

Steve watched in horror as the body that was once his moved in to kill his daughter. He was fighting with everything he had but couldn't do anything. The wolf had complete control now. He could sense it's feral hunger. All he could do was watch as a look of complete horror covered Miranda's face. With tears streaming down her face she raised one little hand to him.

He wanted to close his eyes but couldn't even do that. He wasn't given that much mercy. He was going to have to watch it all.

The werewolf drew back one massive claw and-

"No, bad monster!" Miranda yelled. The scared, sad little girl was gone and in her place was the stubborn little girl that argued about bedtime and about getting a toy every time she went to the store. "Eating people is... not...nice. I've told you before."

The wolf hesitated. Steve felt it's control slacken and he pushed himself forward. Elizabeth had told him that having a pack made the first full moon easier because the alpha could help keep you in control. Steve did not have an alpha, but he seemed to have found his center.

He felt the wolf sinking back into the shadows, defeated. It was still there, it's animalistic urges lingering in the background, but he suddenly found himself in control again. Steve dropped onto all fours in front of Miranda and lowered his head. The little hand that had been reaching out to him before reached up and stroked the hair on top of his head.

"Good monster," Miranda said.

Steve looked up at her. He was still in his wolf form and unable to talk, so instinctively he licked her face. She giggled and he knew everything was going to be alright.

Miranda wrapped her little arms around his hairy neck.

Chapter Twenty Four

The sun broke on a new day and Steve Slate opened his eyes. They were in the cab of the pickup truck and Miranda was sleeping soundly against his side. He patted her gently on her head. He couldn't recall everything that had happened the night before, just bits and pieces. At some point he was pretty sure Miranda had ridden on his back like a pony. When she had gotten tired he had put her back in the truck and huddle down protectively in the mud nearby.

At some point he had changed back into himself and gotten dressed in some loose fitting jeans and a t-shirt he'd picked up at Red's. He couldn't recall that at all.

As he sat silently, contemplating his next move, it occurred to him that he now had surprise on his side. Nobody had expected him to survive the full moon. When Elizabeth and her pack took Owen and Chloe before the elders for whatever farce trial they intended to hold, they would never expect him to come for her. Their guard would be down. All along his hopes and dreams of success had been unrealistic. He had lied to himself and said he could do it, but in the back of his mind he had held onto the fact that no werewolf ever survived their first full moon without a pack.

For the first time since being bitten, he felt better. The ever present wolf wasn't there trying to get out. Last night he had proven his dominance over the beast, and now he was now the master of his own destiny. There was an odd sense of power that came along with it, as if his human body had absorbed some of the wolf's strength.

A bright red tow truck rolled to a stop in front of him and Steve smiled.

One good thing about the Slate family was that

157

they didn't ask many questions. After the tow truck driver helped get the truck out of the mud so he could change the flat, he drove the last few miles to Rick's house. Steve's brother was sitting on the porch picking his guitar, a habit the elder Slate had picked up but never mastered.

"Nice to see ya son," Rick called out to him as he helped Miranda to the ground.

"I appreciate you helping me out," Steve told his brother. "We've got some trouble we need to get out of, and I'd rather not take Miranda along with us."

"No problem," Rick replied. "Mel's got breakfast cooked if you wanna eat with us. I'm sure the girl's will love to spend a day or two with Miranda."

Rick's daughters were, in fact, ecstatic at having another little girl around the house. As soon as they were done eating they took her out in the yard to their playhouse. Mel gathered up the dishes and headed out to watch the kids, leaving the two brothers alone in the kitchen. They sat in silence for several minutes, before Rick finally breached the subject.

"Do you need help?" he asked. "I wont ask you what's going on, but you know if you need me I'll be there for you."

"I think this is something I've got to handle on my own," Steve said.

"Alright," Rick said, and that was that. They spent a few minutes talking about sports and politics, then Steve headed out to tell Miranda goodbye.

"You'll bring mommy with you when you come?"

"Yes," Steve said. He wasn't sure he would make it back, but he wasn't about to tell her. "When I come back to get you I'll bring mommy with me."

"Thank you, daddy," she said, reaching up to hug him. "I love you."

The drive back to Kentucky was uneventful. By early afternoon he was checking back into the same motel where he and Miranda has stayed two nights earlier. He had nowhere to go until nightfall, and he couldn't risk any of the werewolves seeing him out on the street. His only advantage was going to be surprise. He couldn't risk losing that because he was bored or hungry.

As he lay on the bed, flipping through the channels of the motel's out of date television, he started formulating a plan. It was nothing elaborate, just something that he hoped would allow him to slip in unnoticed.

He had no way of knowing that his plans were about to be blown.

Chapter Twenty Five

The sound of voices woke Steve from a pleasant dream. One minute he had been enjoying a quiet afternoon in the park with Chloe and Miranda, and the next he was waking up on the old moth eaten comforter of his motel room bed. In a split second he noticed that the sun was just about to set, Wheel of Fortune was playing on his television and two young men were standing just inside the door to his room. In that same moment instincts he didn't know he had took over, and he sprang off the bed, landing on his feet.

The words that had woke him rang in his ears. *"This is the guy they told us to look for,"* one of them had said. *"We'd better call this is."*

"Or we could just kill him ourselves."

He had been found, but nobody else knew. He didn't consciously decide on a course of action, his body simply reacted. By the time his feet were on the ground, Steve was already charging forward, morphing into the werewolf as he went. The other two men were still staring, dumbfounded.

While still in the middle of his transformation, Steve caught both of the other men by the throat and drove them to the ground. They landed hard enough that the concrete floor beneath the carpet cracked beneath them.

The larger of the two men started to change first. He pushed up with both feet and sent Steve flying backwards. He slammed into the far wall in a cloud of drywall dust, leaving a man sized divot.

The bigger man leapt to his feet and followed, but Steve was ready for him. He lunged forward, meeting his attacker at full speed halfway across the room. They collided with a force that would have killed any human. The two werewolves stumbled away from each other, dazed.

The smaller werewolf was struggling to his feet. He had retrieved a cellphone from his pocket and was feverishly trying to dial a number. Steve knew he couldn't let that call go through. He shoved the other man out of his way and leapt for the phone. Behind him the television exploded and the bigger of the two werewolves collapsed to the floor as a surge of electricity shot through his body.

Steve caught the other man, still in his human form, off guard. The attack was quick and decisive. He landed a blow directly to the man's throat, intending to disable him, but his claws went through meat like a knife through butter. The smaller man's head teetered backwards, then fell to the floor. His phone fell to the concrete between his knees, the call never completed.

The other werewolf had recovered from the electric shock and tried to attack Steve from behind, but he rolled in time to swipe his claws across the other's midsection. The beast let out a yelp and fell backwards, landing in a seated position next to the bed. He was frantically clawing to hold his intestines in even as his body started it's healing process.

As Steve stood his ground, waiting to see what the other werewolf would do next. Instead of attacking again he started to morph back into his human body. After just a few seconds he lay there, a man with a grotesque stomach wound.

"You can kill me, but that doesn't change anything," the man said. "You're wife is going to die soon. The elders already know that she did it. She'll die and Owen Black will be reprimanded but let go. That's how things work, boy."

Steve stalked slowly forward, his jaws hanging open.

"You thought they would kill Owen Black?" the other said with a pained laugh. "He's blood born. You and your old lady are just mutts. They'll kill her and then they'll come for you."

Before he could say another word, Steve ripped his heart out through his chest.

Steve left the two dead bodies in his motel room, along with the room key. Regardless of what happened next, he wouldn't be coming back. He felt a little twinge of guilt at having just snuffed out two lives, but then he thought about what the man had said about his wife and he pushed it aside. The guilt turned to anger. Hatred. It fueled him as he drove from the motel towards Elizabeth's house.

No one paid him any attention when he drove passed the house, unknowingly heading for the same parking spot where Tad Tuttle had parked his rental car two nights earlier. The front lawn looked like they were having a real blowout of a family reunion or party. He counted several dozen vehicles parked on the grass, and even more parked around the looped front drive. The elders apparently didn't travel light. The only thing missing was the people that belonged with the cars. He couldn't see them anywhere.

That must mean they had already moved to the little theater in the clearing, which meant Chloe didn't have much time. He speed up.

Steve hoped the large concentration of werewolves would work in his favor. Elizabeth's men had his sent, but now they would be confronted with the scent of dozens and dozens of strange werewolves. If all worked well they wouldn't notice him until it was too late.

As soon as he shut the truck's engine off he was running, heading straight for the place where the wolfsbane grew. From a hundred yards away he could smell it. He could also faintly smell where Tad Tuttle had entered the woods and he hoped the other man was alright. But he didn't have time to worry about that. He ran straight to the wolfsbane and covered himself in the last of the sickly smelling flowers.

Steve didn't need the clearing, the moon or even his ability to smell to find his way through the forest. A new built in guidance system drove him straight to the front lawn of the house, where he crouched in the bushes and watched to make sure the place really was deserted. When he felt safe, he sprinted across the lawn and took cover behind a parked car. Quickly he worked his way towards the front of the house.

He half expected to find the front door bolted, but he threw it open and stepped inside. Marvin stood at the foot of the staircase, gapping at him.

"Mr. Slate!" the man cried out.

"Listen Marvin, I'm not here to hurt anybody," he said.

"That's a good thing," a female voice said. Instead of Elizabeth, Allison Booth appeared at the top of the stairs. "I would not like to see anyone get hurt, Mr. Slate."

"I'm not leaving here without my wife," he told her. "I don't want to hurt anyone, but I will do whatever it takes to get her out of here."

The young woman walked slowly down the stairs, her arms folded in front of her. Steve didn't want to fight her. She seemed like a nice girl, and apparently the werewolf community needed more of that. He could sense her grandmother's strength in her, but there was something else there as well. Perhaps a little humanity that the other woman didn't posses.

"I don't want to see anyone hurt, Mr. Slate," the girl said as she stepped off the bottom step next to Marvin. "But you must do what you must do. Your wife may have killed my cousin, but it was not her choice. I know that. You know that. The entire council of elders know that. But this is not about guilt. Somebody must pay, and it will never be a pure blood."

Steve just stared at her, not sure of where this was going or what he should do. She could easily be setting a trap for him, but he didn't think so. There was something in her eyes that made him stand his ground.

"Prejudice runs rampant in the lycan community, although you would never hear them admit it," Allison told him. "My mother was born human. She met my father when they were in college and agreed to become like him. What she was not told was that she would never be accepted into our community. She would always be treated like a half-breed. A second class citizen.

"My grandmother believes in this old southern hospitality routine, but just as the old southerners hated their black neighbors, she hates half-breeds. They all do. Even if your wife was totally innocent in Wayne's death, she would still take the fall for it. They'll execute her and pretend that Owen Black is innocent because he was born lycan."

"Then I need to hurry," Steve told her.

"You do," she replied. "I will go back up and stay with the children. Marvin will give you the keys to my grandmother's office and the barn where they are keeping the prisoners. All I can ask is that you try to hurt as few of them as you can. While I do not condone what they believe, they are still my family."

"Thank you, Allison," he said.

"Good luck, Mr. Slate."

Then she was striding back up the stairs. The ser-

165

vant pulled a key ring from his jacket pocket and quickly removed a pair of old worn keys.

"Make sure you take these with you," Marvin said. "I have extras, but if they find these with my scent on them, I'm as good as dead."

Chapter Twenty Six

The key let Steve into Elizabeth's office, but the glass display cases were locked. With no time to waste, he selected a large leather bound book from one of the book cases and smashed through the lids of each case. Feeling a bit awkward, he gathered up the bow and arrows, the Colt .45 and the silver tipped spear. There were six arrows in the case and twelve rounds for the revolver. It wasn't exactly an arsenal, but it was better than walking into the middle of their execution empty handed.

He ran down the steps and back into the yard. The grass was wet as he started around the corner of the house, heading for the barn. He could see the orange glow of a bonfire in the distance and heard multiple loud voiced from that same direction. It sounded more like they were having a party than a trial and execution.

Steve found the front of the barn unguarded, which made him a bit nervous. Despite the silver cage they were in, he didn't think they would leave their two prisoners unguarded. That meant they had already moved them to the clearing. They could be preparing to kill his wife at that very moment.

He stuck the second key into the lock on the front of the building and through the door open. The front door to the cage had been left open. He did not see Chloe or Owen, but there was a large shape laying on the straw in one cage at the back of the barn. As he stood staring at it, Tad Tuttle sat up.

The police detective had seen better days. There was dried blood crusted around his nose and mouth. His jacket was missing and the front of his white shirt was stained with red. One of his eyes was blacked and nearly swollen shut. He smiled, and Steve recognized the look he'd seen on his own face several times over the last few days. Tad might be hurt, but he was angry.

"Looks like you came prepared," Tad said.

"Looks like you've seen better days," Steve said as he raced across the barn. He shoved the key into the door of the detectives cell and opened it. "You can leave. Things are going to get messy around here, you've probably got time to slip off into the night."

"You have to be kidding me," Tad said as he stepped out of the cell. "Those monsters beat me, kidnapped me and then locked me up in the barn with a pair of werewolves during the full moon. There is no way I'm leaving here without getting a little payback."

Tad held out the old Colt and its extra rounds. Tad smiled as he checked the cylinder and shoved the gun into the waistband of his pants. He dropped the extra shells in his hip pocket.

"Just so you know, you're wife came through alright," he said. "Owen Black was taunting her this morning. He said he helped her get through the change so that he could watch tonight when someone called Agleska ripped her heart out."

"Whatever else happens tonight, I want to be the one who kills Owen Black."

The pair stepped out of the barn into the night. Steve had the spear wedged into his belt, and the leather quiver of arrows slung over his shoulder. Tad held the old revolver in both hands. For two men about to walk into the midst of a pack of blood thirsty werewolves, they looked rather ridiculous. They didn't really care.

As they rounded the side of the barn, they could make out the crowd gathered around a blazing bonfire. The little ampitheater area was filled with at least fifty to a hundred bodies, all seeming to sway with the words of a speaker who stood on a raised platform. At the front of the crowd, at the foot of that platform, was a semi-circle of figures in black hooded robes. Chloe knelt in front of the man who was speaking to the crowd.

Steve and Tad zig-zagged their way across the clearing, using trees and the wolf statue to mask their approach. It wasn't perfect cover, if someone had been watching they would have easily been spotted, but for the time being everyone was watching the man on the stage.

"No lycan shall spill the blood of another without provocation!" the man on the stage said. He was a tall, thin man with a pale complication and leathery, almost lizard-like skin. He looked as if he might have been severely burned at some point in the distant past. Steve knew this had to be Agleska - 'the lizard'- Owen's former alpha and Chloe's executioner. "That is the oldest law of our people, yet this woman killed our brother, Wayne Shelley, who was doing nothing more than driving a truck. He was working to support his family and she executed him without remorse."

Steve watched as the crowd reacted. They jeered and hissed at his wife. A few made rude gestures in her direction. All the while, the group of hooded figures at the front stood stoically, their arms folded in front of them.

"Don't take my word for it," the speaker said. "Brother Black, please step forward and address the audience."

Steve's breath caught in his throat as Owen Black emerged from the audience. He was not only free, he looked as if he had just bathed and put on a fresh set of clothes. A few members of the crowd slapped him on the back as he made his way to the front. The man on the stage held out a hand and helped him up to stand next to Chloe.

"I gave Mrs. Slate the gift only a few days ago,"

he said. "She seemed like she would make a good mate, but I know now that she is not what I thought. We encountered Wayne Shelley in the town of Pine Grove, Kentucky. As we were having a conversation, she attacked him from behind without warning. She ripped his heart out and ate it!"

The crowd erupted with anger. Owen paused, letting his accusation sink in, a smirk creeping across his face. Steve drew a silver tipped arrow from his quiver and brought the bow up.

"You've heard it!" the speaker said. "What is the ruling of the council?"

One by one the black clad figures at the front of the crowd held up their hands, thumbs down. The audience behind them cheered. Owen turned towards Chloe and smiled. She was crying. Only twenty feet away now, Steve stepped from behind a tree and took aim at Owen Black's heart.

Then the man who had been doing the speaking reached into his cloak and withdrew a dagger. The silver blade gleamed in the flickering fire light. He moved to stand behind Chloe and raised the knife over his head.

A heartbeat later a silver arrow plunged into his chest. He dropped the knife, took two stumbling steps backwards and topped into the bonfire.

Chapter Twenty Seven

Chaos erupted throughout the crowd. Some of them screamed and ran, while others simply watched in horror as one of their own went up in smoke. The only one who seemed to fully grasp what was going on was Owen Black, who made a dive for the dagger. He was about to pick it up when another arrow struck the wooden platform right in front of his hand.

Steve readied a third arrow as he made a run for the stage. Black seemed to have lost all thought of finishing Chloe off, because he dove to the ground and ran into the panicked crowd.

Before Steve could reach his wife, the black clad group at the front of the crowd turned towards him. Although their faces were hidden in the shadows of their hoods, he could see their eyes glowing orange in the flickering light of the fire. The one closest to him slid her hood back. Elizabeth Shelley snarled at him, the change already washing over her features. She took a step forward and a shot rang out. Steve saw her left shoulder erupt in blood as the bullet tore through her flesh.

Another of the hooded figures moved to intercept him, and Steve took him down with a arrow to the face. At the same moment Tad fired again and dropped the werewolf closest to the stage.

Slowly the remaining members of the pack seemed to be realizing what was happening. Steve could hear the sounds of people undergoing the change all around him, but he had his attention focused entirely on the stage. He released another arrow and eliminated another obstacle between he and his wife. Somewhere off to his right he heard his partner fire again, but he didn't turn to see the results.

He had just reached the foot of the stage when he was blind-sided. The familiar black werewolf hit him hard enough to knock him off his feet. He slammed into the stage hard enough to splinter the wood. Steve lost his grip on the old bow and it went flying into the night. They bounced off the stage and landed in the mud, Owen's snapping jaws only an inch from Steve's face.

"I've had enough of you," Steve snarled. He reached up and drove a thumb into the werewolf's still bloodshot eye. Owen howled in pain but continued his assault.

Steve had lost the bow, but he still had the arrows. He grabbed for one, and Owen lunged. The werewolf's teeth snapped closed only a hair from his throat. At the same time Steve managed to grasp the end of one of the arrows.

With the way they were laying, he did not have a clear shot at Owen's heart, so instead Steve drove the arrow into his creator's shoulder with all his might. The werewolf yelped and jumped backwards.

The clearing had become total chaos. The scent of blood and gunpowder was heavy on the air and people were running in all directions. After seeing the werewolves in action, Tad had thought their chance of surviving were slim to none, but he was starting to believe that they might just make it. Despite their size and strength, the werewolf pack had reacted just as their human counterparts would in the event a surprise gunman started shooting up their gathering.

Tad lost sight of Steve when the big werewolf tackled him. He started to go after them, but another werewolf charged at him. The creature struck him on the run, and together they went flying. But he managed to hold onto the gun. In mid-air he discharged the weapon into the wolf's chest. By the time they landed in the mud, it was already starting to transform back into a human.

As he got to his feet, the night sky seemed to open and it started to pour rain.

Most of the werewolves had fled by that point. Only a few dozen of the hundred or so that had been there in the beginning were left. Most of them had already changed or were in the process of changing. One of the former spotted him at that moment and charged from across the crowd.

Tad took aim, sucking in a quick breath and holding it. At the last possible moment he pulled the trigger. The bullet hit the creature in the forehead, turning it's charge into a slide through the mud. He side stepped out of it's way and started towards the stage.

He was mentally counting his shots as he moved. The old Colt held six rounds, and he had already fired four of them. That meant he had two more shots in the weapon and six rounds in his pocket. Eight shots against twenty-five werewolves didn't seem all that promising.

For the moment, however, none of the werewolves seemed to be paying any attention to him. They were either checking on the wounded or dead members of their packs, or they were watching something going on near the front of the stage.

While none of them were paying attention to him, he popped the four spent cartridges out of the gun and replaced them with fresh rounds.

He reached the backside of the stage and leapt up. Chloe Slate was still where she had been, kneeling with her hands cuffed behind her back. He fished in his pocket and withdrew a set of keys. Tad dropped to the floor behind her and worked to quickly unlock the cuffs.

"You're helping me?" she asked. She was pale and sickly-looking, and didn't seem to recognize him despite having been locked in the cell next to him during the full moon. He wasn't surprised. That had been a long

173

night for her.

"Sworn to serve and protect, ma'am," he said. The handcuffs fell free.

For the first time since they went down, he caught sight of Steve and the black werewolf that had now captured the attention of the crowd. The creature had an arrow sticking out of it's shoulder and was gushing blood. But Steve was still in his human form, so the werewolf had the advantage of size and strength.

"The girl!" someone shouted.

Someone had finally noticed that he had released their intended victim. Suddenly a half dozen of the remaining werewolves were charging at the stage. Chloe began to growl as she started to change.

Chloe had never triggered her change before, but when she saw her husband fighting with Owen Black, it happened on it's own. The anger and hatred of the man who had destroyed their family washed through her entire body. She wasn't sure if she would be able to fight him, because even if he had turned his back on her, he was still her alpha. But she could fight the rest of them. She focused her anger on the werewolves approaching the stage and leapt.

A gunshot rang out behind her, and one of the six approaching werewolves crumpled to the ground. She met the closest of her remaining attackers, a female, at full speed. Chloe caught her around the throat and drove her down into the mud. She heard the cop fire another shot, then she was too lost in battle to be aware of anything else.

The other werewolf was clearly an experienced fighter and had a size advantage, but Chloe was faster and more agile. As the other swung at her face with it's claws, she dodged and delivered a bite to it's neck. Blood flowed into her mouth.

The female wolf screamed.

A second, much larger werewolf hit her from the side, knocking her off of the now bleeding female. Chloe rolled in mid-air, managing to keep herself from being underneath her new attacker when they hit the ground. When they splashed down in the mud they were kneeling several feet apart. They both growled and launched themselves forward.

Tad loaded the last of his spare rounds into the old Colt .45 as he watched the Slates battle the werewolves. He had four shots left, and there were way more than four werewolves still hovering around the clearing.

As one of the creatures positioned itself to double team Chloe, he took aim and fired. The round struck the beast in the stomach. The wound didn't kill it, but it was enough to make the creature cry out and drop back into the shadows.

At last Steve managed to get close enough to the stage to slip out from under Owen and underneath the rough wooden structure. He knew he'd be a better match for the werewolf if he made the change, but he didn't want to give up control. He believed that as long as he held on to his humanity, in the end he'd be able to outsmart his adversary. Elizabeth had even told him as much.

He heard the sound of Tad's pistol discharging multiple times, and out in the rain drenched field he heard the sound of werewolves crying out. He couldn't tell how bad their wounds were, but the silver seemed to drive the fight out of them. The creatures drew back away from the clearing. At last he heard the sound of the Colt's hammer striking an empty chamber, and Tad mut-

175

tering a curse a moment later.

Steve's cover didn't last long, because a moment later Owen lifted the stage into the air and sent it flying towards the Mississippi River. Tad Tuttle landed on his back in the mud a few feet away, the now useless revolver in his hand. One of the other members of the pack seemed to have noticed the now helpless human and moved in to finish him.

Chloe was losing the battle, and she knew it. The other werewolf's size and strength were simply wearing her down. If the cop hadn't kept shooting her would be attackers, she would have lost already. And then she saw Owen destroy the stage, knocking her savior to the ground as he moved in to finish off her husband.

She called out to him, but he didn't hear. He was about to be overtaken. Her own attacker knocked her to the ground and moved in to rip her throat out with his teeth.

Tad was trying to get to his feet when the werewolf made it's run. He had been holding onto the old revolver, but he dropped it in the mud. Just before Owen Black had turned over the stage he had retrieved the arrow that Steve had intended for his creator. As the wolf dove for him he stabbed that arrow out in front of him. It struck the creature in the chest.

As they fell to the ground the shaft of the arrow snapped off, making it impossible to pull out.

He struggled out from under the creature's spasming body as the remainder of the pack began to circle him. This time he really was helpless.

Chapter Twenty Eight

Steve lay on his back and waited, knowing exactly what was going to happen next. The end was at hand. The big black werewolf that was Owen Black stood over him and howled into the rain, announcing his victory to anyone that was listening. Although he didn't know it, it was enough of a distraction that Chloe managed to free herself from her own attacker at the last possible second.

Owen finally looked down at him, and if it was possible, he even smiled. He wanted Steve to know that he was going to die. He wanted to give him a moment to think about it before hand. Then he lunged.

In one quick motion Steve drew the spear from his belt and thrust it upwards. Owen impaled himself on the silver tip, driving his full weight down onto the point. The barbed end cut through his heart, slicing it into multiple mutilated pieces. He let out one week moan as his body began to transform itself back.

"You should have left us alone," Steve said to the human face that was slowly appearing before him. He reached back and found the last remaining arrow in his quiver. "Everybody would have been better off."

A moment later Owen Black hung over him, held up by the handle of the spear, which had driven itself into the muddy ground. Steve stabbed the silver tip of the arrow into the other man's throat, puncturing his jugular. Blood rained down on him as the life faded from Black's eyes.

Steve rolled out from under his creator and jumped to his feet. For the first time since the battle began, he had a chance to survey the scene. The clearing was littered with bloody, wounded and dead bodies. Some of the werewolves were helping their pack mates escape towards the house. Only a hand full remained in

177

the fight, and they were circling nervously.

He saw Chloe and a large brown werewolf panting and slowly circling each other. Only a few feet away two more wolves were moving in on Tad Tuttle who was now unarmed.

"Stop!" a familiar voice boomed.

Elizabeth Shelley appeared out of the rain. Her side was drenched in blood, and she moved with the help of a Miles Smith. The woman truly looked old for the first time. Her rain socked hair clung to the sides of her face.

At her command the clearing fell silent. The other werewolves fell back, allowing Steve, Chloe and Tad to move into a group. The two sides stood leering at each other, everyone showing signs of injury and fatigue. The rain continued to pound them all, turning the clearing into a small lake.

"Do you see what you have done, Mr. Slate?" she asked accusingly. "You've killed or wounded every one on the council of elders. You've slaughtered my children and grandchildren. You've brought death and destruction into our peaceful household."

"I told you to leave my wife alone," Steve snapped.

"You are a monster who must be destroyed," Elizabeth snarled. "A half-breed monster who has no place in this world."

"That's your opinion, but I think you see the monster when you look in the mirror each morning," he told her. "I did not choose this. I did not want this. I was happy living my life as a clueless human. Then one of your people brought us into this. One of your people who you chose to protect because he was one of you."

"I will kill you for this."

"Come on, I'm waiting!" Steve declared.

"Not today," she said after a short pause. "There has been too much blood shed here today. I can't stand to see another member of my family killed. We will bury our dead and then we will hunt you down and kill you, your wife and daughter one by one. Before my life is over I will see you dead and I will eat your daughter's flesh."

"You will never even think of my daughter again," he ordered, a strange feeling of power creeping over him.

He saw the other wolves draw back at the sound of his voice, even Miles Smith. Only Elizabeth stood her ground, but even she appeared shaken.

"An alpha?" she said softly. Then she sighed. "You destroyed your creator, didn't you? You destroyed Owen Black and have taken your place at the head of your pack. Rest assured, that wont save you from me."

"Leave us alone, Elizabeth, and we will never trouble you again," he promised.

"I will never leave you alone," she stated. "I can promise you that. I will not rest until I have destroyed you."

Then she turned back towards the house. Miles took her by the arm and the entire pack started up the hill.

Chapter Twenty Nine

Steve lay on his back and stared at the ceiling of Rick's guest room. The clock on the night stand said it was ten minutes after midnight. It was late October, but the night had turned unseasonably warm, leaving him drenched in sweat. Outside the crickets were chirping in the darkness. He was aware of every sound from the forest and had to fight back the urge to run to the window with every noise.

Beside him Chloe's breathing had slowed as she finally slid into a deep but restless sleep. They had yet to have a conversation about their future, but the thought weighed heavily on both of their minds. They couldn't go home again, not after the way they had left things with Elizabeth's pack and not after having killed or wounded most of the werewolves' council of elders. Tad had assured them that he could handle things with the Miltonboro Police Department and had even accompanied them back to their house to pick up some of their irreplaceable items such as old photos, birth certificates social security cards and family heirlooms. They'd even traded his father's old truck for their personal vehicles. But if they went home and moved back into the same old house, the packs would eventually track them down.

They say that time heals all wounds, and Steve hoped that the saying was true. It wasn't fair to raise their daughter as a fugitive, always on the run from a pack of blood thirsty werewolves. What happened to them hadn't been their fault, but Miranda was the one who truly had to pay the price. She couldn't live a normal life ever again.

In the distance he heard the sound of a limb snapping. He slowly sat up, sure that something about this particular noise was different. He waited, not wanting to wake Chloe until he was sure. They had both been

181

through a lot over the last several days and needed their rest. Hopefully soon they would both be able to sleep through the night without keeping one eye open.

A moment later he heard the sound of multiple sets of feet running through the forest. They were padded feet, but he could hear them as they made their way quickly towards his brother's isolated house. Just as he had thought, Elizabeth had wasted no time in coming after them. The attack on her compound had been an insult to her pride, a sin that could not go unpunished.

Steve reached out and gently nudged Chloe. She sat up quickly, her eyes catching just enough light to shine in the darkness. She was different now. His wife had always been a bit nervous and insecure, but the change had strengthened her resolve. She appeared not only confident, but almost excited about the coming battle. While they might not be able to put their trouble with the packs behind them, this was their chance to make sure the packs thought twice before coming after them.

"They're here," she said, sniffing the air. "Six or seven of them coming in from the north along the shore."

He was impressed by her sense of smell. As they'd prepared for tonight, the two of them had spent the day testing their newfound talents. Steve's hearing was amazing, but Chloe's sense of smell was far beyond his. While blindfolded, she had been able to point out a squirrel, a turkey and even an armadillo that were all over fifty yards from the house. It was an amazing talent.

"The old woman is with them," she said, her voice filled with spite.

They got to their feet and headed for the front porch, hand-in-hand. The pack intended to catch them by surprise, surrounded by their human family members, all of whom were to be pawns in Elizabeth's plans for revenge. What the old woman didn't know was that Rick, his wife and the girls had taken Miranda and went to spend the night in Branson.

But there was one human waiting for them.

Steve and Chloe opened the front door and stepped out onto the porch, still holding hands. They walked to the top step and stood, waiting for the pack members to show themselves. A moment later they did, moving into the front yard clad in dark hooded robes. Elizabeth was in the front, with Miles close by her shoulder. The others were spread out. Among them he saw several of the faces that had been on the search party that found Chloe and Owen's motel.

"What do we owe the honor of your visit?" Steve called out.

"I told you that you would pay for what you did, Steve Slate," the old woman replied.

"You know you brought this all upon yourself," he said. "You know very well that Chloe only killed your grandson because Owen Black told her to. But because she wasn't born into one of your packs, he was supposed to get a pass and she wasn't. Screw that and screw you."

"After the hospitality we showed you, this is how you've chosen to repay us?" she growled. "You violate my house and interrupt a ceremony of the council of elders! You stole family heirlooms and used them to kill members of my family. You slaughtered our elders like they were worthless humans!"

"Worthless humans?" Steve asked. "So there it is, you think being a werewolf makes you better? You think that gives you the right to make decisions for people? To kill anyone that you want?"

183

"I've had enough of this," Elizabeth said. "Kill them all."

A shotgun blast erupted from just over Steve's head. The noise was nearly deafening. Everyone of the pack members flinched, but it was Elizabeth Shelley that dropped to her knees.

Tad Tuttle pumped a second shell into his old twelve gauge and aimed at Miles Smith, who was staring down at the leader of his pack is shock. The shotgun erupted, spraying the big state trooper's midsection with chunks of what had once been Tad's grandmother's silverware. He screamed and fell to the ground, writhing in pain.

Steve had been convinced that the pack would come for them immediately, but it was Tad who had planned the ambush. While the Slates were gathering up their personal items, he had gone to his own house and started loading shotgun shells. He would have preferred to have made silver bullets for his service pistol, but the melting process would have taken to long. Cutting the old forks, spoons and knives into chunks hadn't taken very long at all. And they seemed to work pretty effectively.

On the porch below him, Steve and Chloe took up a pair of shotguns that had been concealed behind a flower planter. They fired, dropping two more of the pack, and then Tad fired again, wounding a fifth. The final member of the pack, who had been hanging back in the trees, stepped forward with her hands raised.

Steve was surprised when Allison Booth stepped out of the shadows. He had not expected her to accompany her grandmother on this quest for revenge. Acting on instinct alone he told Tad Tuttle and his wife to hold their fire. Then he stepped off the porch to greet the final member of Elizabeth's pack.

"I'm not here to fight," the young woman said. "I was here to witness the actions of my grandmother. Her anger and bigotry have taken our family too far off course. I'm glad she did not hurt you or your family again."

The girl stopped over her grandmother, who was growling and clutching at the wounds to her chest and stomach. The chunks of silver weren't buried deep enough below the skin to be fatal, but their poisonous effects on the werewolves were nearly debilitating. The old woman reached up to her granddaughter, pleading for help.

"Elizabeth, I watched my mother plead with you before you killed her," Allison said. "My own father, God rest his soul, broke one of your rules by mistake and exposed the pack. So you killed my mother as punishment!"

"It had to be done," Elizabeth said weakly. "I had to maintain control over the pack. The violation could not go unpunished."

"So you killed my mother, who was innocent?" Allison asked. "My mother, who did everything in her ability to try and please you. Who wanted nothing more than to be welcomed into our family, but was always an outcast because she wasn't pure blood. Well you know what, if my mother wasn't pure, neither am I!"

It happened in an instant, so quick that Tad's human senses couldn't even keep track of it. Allison raised her hand into the air and suddenly sprouted razor sharp claws from the tips of her fingers. In one fatal swipe she ripped Elizabeth's head from her shoulders, sending it rolling into Miles, who cried out in horror. In the same instant her eyes blazed an almost amber color.

When she turned to look back at Steve, the proper girl he had met in the children's play room had returned. She smiled politely.

"I doubt you will be so lucky with the other packs, but the Shelley's shall bother you no more," she said. She looked back at the other members of her pack, all laying wounded on the ground. "Get to your feet!"

One-by-one the other werewolves rose, controlled by the voice of their new alpha.

"Somebody get this bag of bones, it's time to go home."

With tears streaming down his face, Miles Smith gathered up the corpse and head of his aunt and followed Allison Booth into the forest.

Epilogue

With Elizabeth Shelley out of the picture, Miles Smith suddenly became very cooperative. Together he and Tad Tuttle managed to put together a story about the abduction of Chloe Slate and the deaths of Wayne Shelley, Owen Black and Elizabeth Shelley that was somewhat believable. Black, the report said, was actually a black market dealer in exotic and rare animals. When the Slate's accidentally uncovered his secret, he kidnapped the wife and led the husband on a wild goose chase. Officially, Wayne Shelley interfered while trying to save Chloe and got killed. That led Black to the Shelley estate, where he turned the animal on Elizabeth. Tad Tuttle and Miles Smith arrived shortly behind Steve Slate, who had managed to kill Owen Black and rescue his wife. The wolf had, in the process, escaped into the forest.

Shortly after filing his report with the Miltonboro Police Department, Tad turned in his badge and service weapon. The events of the last several days had left him a different man than he had been before. Knowing that werewolves roamed the earth left him questioning everything he knew. Were there more creatures out there? Who was going to protect mankind from them?

He left the police department and drove to a mini storage facility on the edge of town. After his mother had passed away, he had loaded all of her belongings in to a unit and never thought about them until now. Among those were several old boxes of things she had kept that belonged to her parents and grandparents. On a whim he dug those boxes out and started sorting through them in the middle of the gravel lot in front of the storage unit.

He had barely known his grandparents, and he knew absolutely nothing about his great grandparents. His mother had never discussed them, and he had never had any interest in asking questions about them. Now he felt like he had to know. He felt like there was something from his family's past that he needed to know.

Most of what he found was typical family junk, old black and white photos of people he did not and never would know. Pictures of places that he would never see or visit. These were things that a museum curator might be interested in seeing, but they meant nothing to him. Until he reached the end of the very last box. Tucked into the bottom was a small leather satchel.

Tad pulled the bag out and looked it over. His first thought was that it resembled a doctors black bag, and as he looked closer he saw that he was right. Inscribed on the handle was the name: *Dr. J. L. Tuttle M.D.* But what he found upon opening the bag was not the typical wares of a medical doctor. Instead, what he found was a stash of horror movie props.

He sorted through the container, separating the items into piles. In the end he had counted out three wooden stakes, two elaborate crucifixes, three vials of strange looking fluids and a few dozen .45 rounds tipped with silver bullets. The pistol rounds were an identical match for the ones he had used in Wickliffe.

Thanks to the wonders of the internet, it didn't take long to track down information on Dr. J.L. Tuttle. An old edition of the Pine Grove Gazette told of how cholera had struck the nearby town of Miltonboro hard in 1845. Tuttle, who was a Miltonboro native and recent medical school graduate, fought hard to save his towns-people, but the fight was in vain. Of the town's 700 residents, 512 succumb to the disease, including his wife and two of his three children. The lone survivor was Ellis Tuttle, Tad's great grandfather. Survivors had "sworn to rebuild".

Dr. J.L. Tuttle's name was mentioned in a 1856

article in The Oregon Argus. The article told of how residents of a small village near Oregan City had began to suffer from a bizarre illness in early 1855, four years after the official end of the cholera outbreak that had killed 150,000 nationwide. Some residents believed it was the disease making a comeback, while others claimed that the area was besieged by witchcraft or dark magic.

A group of mysterious 'doctors' arrived on the scene. They didn't hold office hours or even see a single patient, but they swore to rid the community of it's illness. The group stuck mostly to themselves, sleeping during the day and roaming the countryside at night. Two days following the death of the final victim, the group disappeared.

The last reference he found of his great great grandfather was a clipping from a Paducah paper. There was no date and the name of the newspaper was not included on the website. Dr. J.L. Tuttle and his son, Ellis, now a young man, had arrived in the Paducah area to 'investigate' the death of an unnamed young boy. A local doctor reported that the boy had died from a wolf attack, although the reporter pointed out that it had been years since the last wolf in the area had been trapped and killed.

Two more death's followed the doctor's report, all of which were credited to a 'very large wolf'.

Dr. Tuttle had sworn that he would catch the animal responsible for the deaths, but after six days he himself vanished. Ellis had waited an additional week for his father to return, but he was never seen again. Following the doctor's disappearance, there were no further wolf attacks reported.

As Tad sat staring at the computer screen, he suddenly knew what he was meant to do. His next search was for werewolf and vampire hunters, something that he would have said was ridiculous only a week earlier.

The pickup threw up a cloud of dust as it rumbled down the old gravel road. It was surrounded on all sides, for nearly as far as the eye could see, by grassy swamp land. Here and there an old grizzled tree sprang up through the muck and mire, but mostly it was just wetlands. Occasionally an alligator would pop up on the surface, then vanish back into the murky water. The air was hot and humid, even with the AC pumping at full blast.

Eventually they came to a fork in the road. Steve Slate paused before proceeding on the eastern branch of the road. He didn't really know if it was instinct or his heightened senses that was driving him, but he had no doubt that he was going the right direction. He knew they were taking a big gamble, but they needed a big payout to keep their little family safe. Allison had promised that the Shelley's were through with his family, but he had every reason to believe that the other packs would want revenge.

As the drove, more trees began to pop up around them, and soon they found themselves in an almost wooded area. The swamp began to look more like the Louisiana Bayou and less like a Florida wetland. The gravel road soon became a dirt road, and then little more than a trail. Weeds slapped at the underside of the truck and tree branches pinged off the radio antenna.

"Are you sure we're going the right way?" Chloe asked.

"I'm sure," he told her.

The trail made a hard ninety degree turn, dropped through a ditch with green water standing in it and then headed straight into a row of Magnolia trees. Those trees seemed very out of place in the middle of a swamp, and they were lined up along each side of the old road. But they had grown wild and unkempt, nearly making the road impassable. Branches brushed against the side mirrors and scratched at the windows as they made their way slowly through them.

Passing through the Magnolia trees was like going through a magical door and coming out in Wonderland. On the far side of the trees, the swamp made way for a manicured lawn that led up a slight incline to a house. It was nothing like the Shelley's riverside mansion, but it was a large brick home that seemed out of place in the middle of the swamp. A pickup was parked under a carport, and down by the waters edge, where the lawn met the swamp, a fan boat was anchored to a concrete post.

"He's here," Chloe suddenly said under her breath. They exchanged a quick look as Steve pulled his truck to a stop near the house. "And he's coming this way fast."

Steve took a deep breath and climbed out of his truck. He couldn't smell the approaching man, his scent was lost in the smells of the swamp, but he could feel his presence. He was approaching quickly, on foot, through the swamp. Steve turned in that direction, waiting, not knowing if death or a possible ally was on it's way.

The form that immerged from the water was like something out of a nightmare. It was neither man nor werewolf, and it was covered from head-to-toe in slimy green swamp sludge. It came, walking at first on all fours, and then raising up on it's hind legs as it's feet reach dry land. It growled, a low threatening sound. The creature bared it's teeth, letting Steve know that his presence wasn't welcomed here.

Chloe moved around to his side, which only pushed the creature farther. It dropped into a crouch and began to stalk towards them. Steve grabbed his wife's hand and squeezed, trying to reassure her, although he was suddenly feeling a little less than confident. The creature's growl grew louder, more threatening.

Suddenly Miranda appeared around the front of the truck. Somehow she had managed to wiggle out of the seat belt and get out of the truck. She giggled as she moved passed her parents towards the bizarre creature. Chloe tried to grab her, but Steve pulled her back. His daughter was not a werewolf, but he believed she had a skill of her own.

"Hello monster," she said, holding a hand out to the creature.

The creature stood perfectly still for a long moment. Then a human face began to emerge from behind the mess of swamp sludge and fur. To everyone's surprise, the Moon Dog was smiling. He reach his hand out to Miranda's.

Afterword

First of all I need to thank my wife and daughter, who standby me despite my shortcomings and my passion for writing scary stories. They are my inspiration and the reason I keep going.

Then there is Maisie Schneider, the proof reader who somehow got tasked with making me not look like an idiot. It's tough work, but she's done a good job. We don't always agree on changes, but she isn't afraid to make suggestions.

Thanks to Sheila Hughes, my mother, for supporting my writing dream through the years and for being the one who instilled a passion for the written word in me.

I also, surprisingly, need to thank Jay Bonansinga. I never thought I would befriend a New York Times Best Selling Author, or anyone associated with The Walking Dead, but fate managed to bring us together for a literary event in the fall of 2014. Jay is not just an awesome author, he is also a pretty good guy to hit up for advice. And he writes a pretty mean recommendation! Thanks Jay!!!!

ALSO AVAILABLE FROM
Matthew Alan Hughes

THE GHOST
IS THE
MACHINE

AN ANTHOLOGY OF STEAMPUNK INSPIRED GHOST STORIES

FEATURING A STORY FROM STOKER AWARD WINNING
NYTimes BESTSELLING AUTHOR
JOE HILL
EDITED BY PATRICK SCALISI

Preditors and Editors 2012 Anthology of the Year

ANTHOLOGY

MON CŒUR
MORT

MY DEAD HEART
AN ANTHOLOGY OF NEW HORROR FICTION

POST MORTEM PRESS

ANTHOLOGY

ANTHOLOGY

NOVEL

NOVEL

SHORT STORY COLLECTION

Find out more about Matthew Alan Hughes @:
https://www.facebook.com/mahughes.horror